FAE'S WITCH
FATED MATES OF THE FAE ROYALS, SUMMER COURT BOOK 5
HELEN WALTON

Walton House Publishing

CONTENTS

Foreword   1

Epigraph   3

1. Pepper   4

2. Lorcan   14

3. Lorcan   24

4. Pepper   34

5. Lorcan   46

6. Pepper   55

7. Pepper   65

8. Lorcan   70

9. Pepper   77

10. Lorcan   90

11. Lorcan   97

12. Pepper   104

13. Lorcan   108

14. Lorcan   118

15.	Pepper	122
16.	Pepper	128
17.	Lorcan	137
18.	Pepper	144
19.	Lorcan	150
20.	Pepper	155
21.	Lorcan	161
22.	Pepper	169
23.	Pepper	174
24.	Lorcan	180
25.	Lorcan	186
26.	Pepper	193
27.	Lorcan	200
28.	Pepper	210
29.	Lorcan	215
30.	Lorcan	226
31.	Pepper	234
32.	Lorcan	241
Bonus scene		247
Acknowledgments		249
Also By		250
About Author		253

FOREWORD

AUTHOR NOTE

Choosing character names is not always easy, and there are times you pick them to mean something for the character and the story. I've included the pronunciation and meaning of the names, and if you're like me, and like to know and still pronounce the names the way you read them, then welcome to my club.

Niamh pronounced neeve meaning radiance.

Fintan pronounced fin-tan meaning white fire.

Eamon pronounced aim-on meaning keeper of riches.

Maeve pronounced may-veh meaning intoxicating.

Diarmuid pronounced deer-mid meaning without enemy.

Orlaith pronounced or-lah meaning golden princess.

Rian pronounced ree-an means little king.

Briana pronounced bree-a-nah meaning noble.

Aislinn pronounced ash-lin meaning a vision or dream.

Saoirse pronounced seer-sha meaning freedom.

Lorcan pronounced lor-can meaning silent or fierce.

Ciara pronounced kee-ra meaning dark.

Roisin pronounced row-sheen meaning little rose.

Donagh pronounced done-acka meaning brown-haired warrior.

Deirdre pronounced deer-dree meaning broken-hearted.

Malachi pronounced mal-lah-key means messenger of God.

Fallon pronounced fa-len meaning descended from a ruler.

Ailbhe pronounced all-bay meaning white.

Tadhg pronounced tie-guh meaning poet or philosopher.

For the warrior
will battle the
flames for love.

CHAPTER ONE
PEPPER

"S TOP SQUIRMING," I SAID, resisting the urge to roll my eyes at the woman.

The woman believed a demon had possessed her husband, but every supernatural creature understood demons didn't possess humans. They looked down on them as though they were nothing but fuel for their powers, which they were. Humans were also good to use for money, which we witches did a lot. It was easy to convince humans to part with their money for potions and elixirs. Everyone wanted a cure for everything.

Supernatural creatures were harder to come by these days. They were all in hiding since the Fae King sealed the Veil and chaos had ensued in the wake of his revenge. Grandmother told stories of the time passed down to her through the generations before she'd died of old age. She'd weaved so many stories, it was like I'd lived through it, too.

Witches had renamed themselves healers. Nowadays, we were called alternative healers. The human fools didn't realize the forms of healing they'd manufactured in laboratories were the alternative ones. Chemicals were far worse cures than the natural ingredients I used. People didn't believe in magical powers any longer.

"Please," the woman begged.

I think her name was Omar. No, that wasn't right. It didn't matter. I wouldn't be in India for much longer. A demon hadn't possessed her husband. He was a straight-up cheater and was trying to worm his way out of it by saying he wasn't himself. Too bad for the rogue I saw straight through his lies, but his poor wife was superstitious and holding onto the belief a demon forced her husband into the arms of another woman.

"Don't worry," I said, flinging back my dark cloak. Sure, the cloak was old school according to our history, but witches dated back forever, way before my time, and the cloak was warm. "I have the perfect potion right here to rid the demon from your husband."

"Thank you," she sobbed, wringing her hands together in prayer mode.

As for God... well, I didn't have any proof of his existence yet.

The husband's gaze snapped toward my face, belying the fact he was dishonest. There was a startled wideness in his pupils that showed he was deceitful, plus there was a darkness I sensed in him through the magic vibrations in the air. I despised liars. Why didn't people admit to their faults and failures? Life would be easier for all if they did. I suppose I wouldn't have as much work as I did now. Then I wouldn't have as much money.

"Right," I said, getting over my little gloominess because money helped.

I wasn't greedy, as others claimed witches were. Practical. Money bought things. Important things. Sure, I liked a little luxury alongside the important items. So what if this cloak cost a lot of money and I had to fly to Paris to purchase the expertise of a Parisian witch to help me make it? Well worth the money and the trip. It wasn't just a statement piece. The cloak had a practical purpose.

My fingers searched through the vials in the pouch secured around my waist. I recognized them all by touch since I stored each potion in a different vial for easy identification. When I came to these types of calls, I carried the most used ones with me. Hence, I found the one I was looking for, a vial with a rounded bottom and a long skinny neck. I almost laughed as I pulled it free and brandished it under the fluorescent lights in their kitchen like I'd drawn Excalibur from the stone. Inside the glass vial, the liquid swirled an ominous brown-black color like a dirty puddle of oily water. It'd taste worse than filthy water.

"What's that?" the man asked, apprehension coming through his voice.

He probably believed I was a joke. Someone his wife found online who was taking her money in a scam. It was easier advertising these days and earning more money by taking jobs from the public even if most were skeptics, but I always took these things seriously. That's why the potion might look like filthy water and taste horrid, but he would never cheat again with the magic I'd imbued into the liquid.

I peered at him from under my thick lashes. "A potion to rid you of the demon. Then you'll never cheat on your wife again."

His lips pulled into a tight grimace.

Like I assumed. He understood he was in the wrong but wouldn't admit it. I placed the vial on the Formica kitchen table and slid my hand back into the pouch. The metal handcuffs were warm from sitting next to my body for so long. I yanked them free and dangled them in his face.

"First, we put these on."

He jerked back with a start. "What for?"

"Demons can be difficult to remove. It will resist my efforts and we don't want you hurting your wife by accident while we do it. Do you?" I raised my eyebrows.

His wife stepped forward and rubbed his shoulder. The amount of love this woman had for this two-faced piece of scum made me sick to my stomach. She'd see through him in a minute. The potion was part truth serum. I longed to see his face once he started telling her the truth.

"Ah, no." He squinted at his hands resting on the table.

I slapped the handcuffs on his wrists. They wouldn't stop him from hurting us, but it would give him the illusion we were in control. It was more often than not enough in these circumstances because he was a weak-willed man.

"What next?" he asked.

"I pour the potion into your mouth, and you swallow it. Easy. Right?"

"Is that all?" He leaned back in his chair as though my words were trivial. Meaningless. As though nothing would happen. Smug. The word fit him to a 't'. He grated on my last nerve.

This man put me off relationships. I'd seen too many humans behave appallingly to those they say they loved.

"Mm-hmm." I picked up the vial and popped the cork. A putrid odor wafted from the brownish-black liquid.

He attempted to shove his chair back, but I grabbed the handcuffs and yanked him forward with enough force, he let out a startled yelp. I shoved the open vial into his mouth and poured it inside. He gagged. I slammed a hand over his mouth, pinching his nose shut with my thumb and forefinger too. He had no choice but to swallow the offensive liquid or risk suffocating. Twenty seconds ticked by before he gulped the liquid and gasped for air. I let go of his face and the handcuffs. In an overdramatic fashion, he poked his tongue out and wiped it on the back of his hands.

"Is that it?" the wife asked.

"Now it's time for the spell."

"Wait. You said nothing about a spell," he said.

"Didn't I? I guess I forgot." I cackled. "Your wife is the one paying, so I guess it's up to her if I proceed with removing the demon."

"Yes, please, do it," she said.

"Demon's plunder.

Soul to soul.

Tell us the truth.

No more lies.

Forever more."

The man scrambled to his feet. His mouth opened and closed as though he wanted to talk but didn't at the same time.

"Yusuf, are you all right?" his wife asked.

"Amara, I did you wrong."

That was her name!

"I lied. There is no demon. I cheated on you with my own free will." He slapped both hands over his mouth, making the handcuffs clink.

I gathered my used vial and stuffed it back into my pouch.

Amara gasped and clutched her chest.

Her husband turned to me. "You witch!"

"Yeah, yeah," I muttered because I was a witch.

"Undo the spell." He launched himself at me, but I sidestepped his clumsy attack, and he landed face-first on the floor.

"Sorry, only your wife can ask me to undo the spell since she paid for my services. Amara, would you like me to remove the spell?"

Amara's gaze hardened on her husband. "No. Leave it. I have more questions for my husband."

"Awesome," I said with a knowing smirk. "I'll leave you the key for the handcuffs. They come with the price of the spell."

I rummaged in my pouch for the small key to the handcuffs, found it buried in the corner, and tossed it at Amara. She caught it with a calculating glint in her eyes.

"Thank you, Pepper." She twirled the silver key under the fluorescent lights like it held the answer to all her questions in life.

I hoped it would answer the questions she had about her deceitful, cheating husband.

"My pleasure." I swirled my cloak around me in dramatic fashion and left with a puff of smoke from a hidden smoke bomb I'd tossed onto the floor.

My phone rang, destroying my magical exit and making me seem all too human and not made of magic.

I wasn't.

Witches were humans with abilities to cast spells. I wasn't like the other supernatural creatures who existed around the world. Such as a wolf shifter, for example, who shifted forms from human to wolf and back again. They also scented lies and their mates. The wolf shifter calling me right now had scented his fated mate in a Fae. A Fae princess, no less. The Fae were elusive to the point they only existed in the Summer Court, but her appearance and another Fae princess's appearance on Earth signaled a change.

I might not possess powers like others, but I sensed things. Seen things in my dreams I'd never mentioned to anyone. There was no one I'd trust those dreams to.

Sledge's name flashed across the screen. I didn't answer his call, even though I grasped why he was calling. I'd avoided returning to Crystal Creek for months now. All because of what I'd dreamed.

The call ended and started again. I waved down a taxi and climbed inside, asking for the airport. My phone quietened, then rang again. An hour later, he hadn't relented. The ringtone annoyed the ever-living hell out of me. I should turn my phone off, but what if another client called?

"What?" I snapped into the phone.

"Pepper, so nice of you to answer."

"I'm busy, Sledge."

"Yes, you're always busy these days, but I need your help."

"I've helped you a lot of late."

When someone had attacked his father and mortally wounded him, he'd called me for help. I'd been willing, since a long time ago our families were related. Now it was distant enough that no one else identified us as family and, since a witch could only control magic and didn't possess it, we never inherited the traits of supernatural creatures. A witch and wolf shifter offspring could never shift into a wolf. Plus, Sledge paid well.

"I'm grateful, but there's more."

"There always is." I sighed.

The lure of working for the supernatural community was appealing. I was tired of helping humans with their petty grievances. I longed to try my powers on something grand.

"Pepper," his voice softened. "Are you all right?"

I kept my focus on the here and now instead of the horrifying dream plaguing me over the last few months. The softness of his voice made me want to see him, for the fact he was a member of my distant family. I didn't have many family members left. Not that my family was close by any means.

"I'm fine," I said, snapping iron into my spine. "But I'm busy. I can't come."

He chuckled. "Remember, wolf shifters hear lies."

Damn.

"I suppose I can come now, since I don't have another client booked."

"Thank you. I'd appreciate that a lot."

"Yeah, yeah," I said, paying the taxi driver and walking into the airport.

Contrary to what people believed, witches didn't fly on broomsticks. I'd tried with many spells, but balancing on a thin broom handle was nigh on impossible while zooming through the sky.

"When can I expect you?"

I checked the flight times on the board. Just my luck, a flight to Australia left in a few hours. Was I destined to go there now? I shook my head. Fate. I tried not to think too hard about it.

"It will take at least twenty-four hours for me to get there from India."

"What are you doing in India?"

"Working, of course."

"I should have known. Don't worry, I intend to pay you when you help us here."

"I still haven't collected my debt from the last time I helped you," I said. "Are you planning to trade more favors?"

"No. I still owe you two favors."

"That's right, you do. One for helping Arrow when the Fae King had frozen him in a block of ice. The other for helping your father," I said. "I guess I have more reason to come now."

"Great," Sledge drawled. "I'll see you tomorrow."

I hung up the phone. Two favors from the Alpha wolf shifter of Crystal Creek. Would they be enough to help me if my dream came true?

CHAPTER TWO
LORCAN

THE LEATHER-BOUND GRIMOIRE WARMED in my palms. It always did because once I opened the pages, I spent hours searching through the contents. The spells and potions, the history of the witch family the grimoire belonged to. The magic inside the book drew me to it time and time again. Even though I fooled myself into pretending the only reason I searched the contents was because of the potion I'd drank. I closed the cover and traced my finger over the etched willow tree. Even in my sleep, the image was familiar. I could draw the image with my eyes closed if I was artistic, like my sister Roisin.

I stepped inside the massive fireplace in my bed chambers, wriggled a large brick free, and placed the grimoire safely back in its hiding spot. Father knew I had the book, but no one else in the family did, and I wanted to keep it that way. Witches were instrumental in aiding the Trappers. I despised them for it. So would every Fae.

A resounding knock on my door had me shoving the brick back into place. I dusted off my hands, even though there'd been no fire in the fireplace for centuries. Hurrying over to the door, I flung it wide.

Ciara stood in the doorway. I wasn't expecting my sister so soon, but I was glad she'd come to see me before I left for Earth.

She glanced over her shoulder, then faced me. "I have found nothing yet."

My older brother had potentially found a place on Earth connected to our dwindling Spring of Life, but powerful magic protected the place. Rian had tasked Ciara with researching the library for answers.

"I thought you'd find something in your books about what Rian found behind the waterfall."

"Malachi and I have been searching, but we can't find the book he remembered reading about the stone pillars."

"I can look while I'm on Earth."

"No. From what Rian said about the poisoned darts, it's not safe," she said. "Besides, you'll need all your focus on Saoirse if you're to convince her to come home."

Footsteps echoed down the marble hallway. Ciara glanced over her shoulder again. Father's robes swirled into view. His steps didn't falter as he scanned Ciara's face, then stepped beside her.

The Fae King stared at me. His indigo-rimmed blue eyes were like looking into a mirror.

"Is it time already?" I asked.

"I'd assumed you'd be eager to see Saoirse," Father said.

"She knows how to take care of herself. If you're so concerned, why don't you see her yourself?"

I couldn't keep the bite out of my words after Father banned her from returning to the Summer Court when she'd mated with a wolf shifter. His reaction was out of character since our fated mate was destined for us, and we didn't have a choice about who that person would be.

"I would, but she's liable to gut me again." He half smiled, half grimaced.

Our father was a complicated Fae to read. He kept a lot of his emotions to himself, but he was proud of our fighting skills. Skills I'd rather forget after the deaths I'd doled out with my sword. I closed my eyes to will those images from my mind, but they never disappeared. They haunted me day and night. How did he live with all the blood on his hands?

"Can you blame Saoirse for the way she reacted?" I mumbled.

"Lorcan." He sighed.

I opened my eyes. "Let's go."

"Wait." He placed a hand on my shoulder. "I worry about you. All of you."

"I see you do, Father. The others might not be as close to you as I am, but you have to let us go at some time. You can't keep us locked in the Summer Court forever. We're already suffering because of it."

He glanced away. "I wanted no one to suffer. It's why I locked the Veil."

My lips parted, but he held up his hand, sensing my rebuttal.

"It's also why I created the doorway. A way for Fae to travel to Earth where we can keep track of them. I want to prevent what happened in the past from occurring again."

"No one wants to see Fae burned at the stake."

Ciara gasped. She was a babe in our mother's womb when those atrocities had occurred and hadn't witnessed the scenes. I was glad Ciara and Roisin hadn't seen the horrors. They were sweet and innocent.

Father's eyes met and held mine. The night we'd found both my grandparents burned to death was forever ingrained in our minds. The sight. The scent. The horror. Then seeing my mother and two of my sisters on fire. I battled against the churning emotions in my chest. Father understood. The same emotions were reflected at me in his eyes. The nightmares haunted us both. We'd saved Mother, Aislinn, and Briana. Then we'd gone on a killing spree, ending the lives of the Trappers who'd sought to take our powers. The Trappers had believed they could take a Fae's power by burning us.

I rubbed a finger over my hip bone. After our witch aide, Saltine, gave me a potion to give me the ability to track the Trappers, a small red mark appeared. I'd never shown it to anyone in my family over the many centuries since that night. I didn't comprehend what it meant, and I had found nothing in her grimoire to help me understand the mark. Had her potion changed me forever? Could I still track Trappers? Not that I needed to since we'd killed every one of them.

"The night." Father swallowed.

"I don't want to talk about it."

"I understand." His crown of thorns writhed around his head, which always happened when he grew agitated. "I don't enjoy talking about it either."

Silence descended between us. A nightingale landed on the windowsill and broke into song.

Father's lips pulled into a smile. "The night I met your mother, I coaxed a nightingale to sing. She danced with me in the forest under the moonlight and fireflies joined us. There were so many special moments the first night we met. I have them embedded in my heart forever. I use those bright memories to combat the dark ones. When you find your fated mate, she'll bring you the brightness you're lacking."

Mother and Father had told us the story of the night they'd met many times over the years. How Mother's voice used to trick men into thinking they were her mate, but not Father. He recognized she was his. Her powerful voice didn't trick him.

"You think I'll find my fated mate?" I stepped into the hallway.

Father dipped his head. "I do. I'd given up hope, but not now that Saoirse and your brother Rian have found theirs."

He was unaware Briana had found her fated mate with a wolf shifter, too. Father's attitude toward returning to Earth had only just changed, and Briana was worried about telling him after his overreaction to Saoirse upon discovering her fated mate was a wolf shifter. Briana would have to tell him soon. A fated mate was a hard secret to keep, even if Rian had kept his secret for ten years.

"I don't want one," I lied.

Father scoffed.

"Why would I? I'm enjoying all the Fae women trying to get me to choose them."

Ciara laughed.

He rubbed his forehead. "It was foolish of me to tell you all to choose a mate. Fated love is worth waiting for."

"Love?" I shook my head. "No thank you."

The damage ran deep within me, so much so it would be impossible for a woman to love me. What woman would want a killer?

"I'll talk to Saoirse for you."

"Thank you, Lorcan."

The door closed behind me, and for some strange reason, it felt like this would be the last time I stood inside the room. Each step along the marble hallways of the Summer Court palace felt as though it was my last. When I was younger, Saoirse and I, being the closest in age, had run through the palace playing. Those years seemed so long ago. Everything had changed. We'd been so carefree back then, believing nothing and no one would harm us. We were immortal and invincible. Then we weren't. The Trappers had a lot to answer for.

"I realize you've been sneaking to Earth like your brother and sisters," Father said.

Since it wasn't a question, I didn't bother answering him.

"Have you sensed any Trappers during your time there?"

"No, I haven't."

His shoulders sagged under the length of his thick cloak. The Fae King never changed in appearance, but his age shone through the depths of his eyes. I perceived the changes as I detected them in my eyes when I studied my reflection in the mirror. The heaviness in our hearts shone through the blue depths like a deep ocean of pain and suffering while the indigo rim lit it with love for our family.

Grier, Father's aide, opened the palace doors and followed us outside into the warm breeze. Magic filled the Summer Court. Every step on the soil with my bare feet grounded me in the magic of our realm. Power filled my body and vibrated, longing to free itself. What I wouldn't give to release it all in one burst to see what would happen. Instead, I harnessed my power. I'd controlled my power to the point of suffocation since we were in the utopia of the Summer Court. With so many Fae in the kingdom, we all used our powers. Trees grew to spectacular heights. Their limbs flourished with leaves. Wildflowers dotted the distant hills in a dazzling display of colors. The forever summer sky was a vibrant blue with pure white fluffy clouds that looked soft enough to sleep on. Fields of gormberries bloomed and fruited on regular occurrence, keeping us sustained with our second favorite fruit. Blueberries on Earth were our first favorite. Gormberries were similar but not as sweet, no matter how much power we infused into the plants. There wasn't much left to do for everyone. But even though our powers were elemental, they were useless in curing our languishing Spring of Life.

We trekked the long walk from the palace to the tower the Fae King had ordered constructed to contain the doorway through the Veil. Past the village and through the fields of our version of what humans called wheat. Our crop was called cruit. We ground it into sweet flour and made the most delicious loaves of bread and cakes. Food I'd miss while on Earth. There was a lot I'd miss, including the long line of Fae women willing to compete to become my mate. Their enthusiasm helped to ease the burden of this secluded existence. Gave me solace from my dark memories.

We reached the tall tower surrounded by royal guards in their red attire. Mother stood in all her regal finery talking to a pair of guards as though they weren't beneath her. Her heritage of Earth-living Fae had brought us closer together. She lifted her head and smiled at Father in a way that made me want a woman to smile at me with love and affection. Her gaze lifted to me, and her petite brows puckered. She strode over to us and wrapped me in a hug.

"Be safe, my son."

I embraced her. There was always a special warmth from my mother's hug. Her arms soothed any ache of the mind or body.

"I will," I promised her and kissed her cheek.

We drew apart, but her appraising eyes missed nothing. Her lips pressed into a tight line as though she was preventing herself from saying what was on her mind. Father slid his arm around her waist and drew her to his side. His touch mellowed her, for she molded into him and let out a deep breath.

"I'll be back as soon as I can," I said.

The words rang empty, even to my ears. Father dipped his chin. The tension in his body escaped through his powers, making his hands glow. Mother placed her hands over his, accepting all of him for who he was.

I longed for a love like theirs, but I turned from the sight to my sister.

"Bye, Ciara."

She threw her arms around my neck and whispered into my ear, "Remember what I said. Stay away from the waterfall."

I walked toward the tower. The two guards, Patrick and Declan, who were accompanying me, nodded at my arrival. I didn't want them to come, but Father insisted anyone going through the Veil had an armed escort. His overprotectiveness was stifling, as always. A scribe opened a book and wrote all our names on the parchment. Another new system to keep track of which Fae traveled to Earth. Father was thorough in his protection of the Fae.

Another guard opened the door to the tower. Inside the doorway, the Veil swirled like a vortex. Power swarmed my hands in a blue-green glow, calling to the tumultuous Veil. I lifted my hands and coaxed the Veil back to a calm curtain. The guards appeared uncertain, but now the doorway was calm, it was time for us to step through to Earth. They hadn't ventured to Earth since the fateful night of the Trappers' destruction. They'd been a part of the death, and I'd spent a lot of time in the guards' ranks after that night.

Patrick and Declan were close friends. They understood me in a way my siblings no longer did. The anxiety at crossing the Veil back to Earth swam through all of us. I'd broken through the locked Veil by myself many times over the years, but today seemed different.

Momentous.

A day that would change everything.

CHAPTER THREE
LORCAN

P ATRICK STEPPED FROM THE Veil before me, his sword hand twitching as though he expected an attack the moment he stepped foot back on Earth. I placed a calming hand on his shoulder and urged him to the side. Earth had changed since they were last here. In a lot of ways, for the worse. Humans no longer believed in us. They wouldn't form a group to destroy us because they didn't realize we existed.

"It's safe, Patrick," I said.

"How can you be sure?" he asked, head whipping left and right, taking in every direction a threat might come at us.

I'd never told them of me and my siblings' travel through the locked Veil. We'd kept the secret from our parents. Now wasn't the time to tell them, either. The secret would be ours always, more than ever now the Fae King had opened a doorway. I wouldn't risk him changing his mind once again.

"I'd sense a Trapper if one existed. Remember?"

Saltine had never said her potions would wear off, and I'd found nothing in her grimoire to say they would either.

"Right," Declan said, stepping through the Veil and lifting his glowing palms to shut it. "Lorcan drank a witchy voodoo potion. It will alert him to Trappers like it did that night."

"Aye."

Patrick's shoulder relaxed under my palm, so I released my grip.

"There's nothing to sense. We killed them all," I said.

More times than I cared to admit, I said a silent plea to let that be true.

"Which way?" Declan asked.

"Left."

Passing through the Veil was no longer an exact method of travel, as it had been back in our free days. I'd focused my mind and energy on Saoirse, hoping the power in the Veil would deliver us to her location on Earth. If it hadn't, then we'd be searching for a while. Earth was a lot larger than the Summer Court. So much so, I was glad for Saltine's potion all those years ago. Otherwise, we'd never have found all our adversaries.

We'd come through the Veil beside a lake. The expanse of water glistened under the warmth of the glowing golden sun. The lake appeared healthier than the one in the Summer Court. Ever since our Spring of Life had dwindled, our lake had lessened, too. No one outside of the royal family recognized the plight of our spring, but they all understood the Summer Court was no longer our utopia.

While here on Earth, I intended to search for answers much like Saoirse had endeavored to do in her travels to this realm. Even her great power over water had found no answers to explain why our spring was slowing.

I walked across the sandy soil alongside the lake. Patrick, always the protector, strode in front of me, leaving footprints in the sand with his bare feet.

"Patrick, give it a rest. The Fae King isn't here to question your diligence. Besides, I can protect myself."

I'd protected myself for centuries. Learned many weapons. Martial arts too.

"But we are under strict orders," he said.

"Aye. You are guards, but you can guard me from my side. You don't need to smother me. I've had enough Fae women trying to smother me in their quest to become a royal."

Patrick and Declan chuckled.

"As if you're complaining about all the women," Declan said.

"'Tis a hardship." A grin stretched my lips.

"I should hope it's hard, otherwise they'd be very disappointed," Declan ribbed, elbowing me in the side.

Laughter flowed between us. This was better. They were more relaxed now and less on guard for the nonexistent threat. From what Briana had told me, this town was owned by wolf shifters and protected by witches' magic. Humans didn't come here and if they did, the magic made them want to move on. She'd also told me of her fated mate, the Alpha wolf, Sledge. When I'd learned she'd accepted him, it had been a shock, but I suppose we were all shocking each other these days. Saoirse had mated with a wolf shifter and fallen pregnant. Rian had met his fated mate and kept her a secret for ten years, torn between his duty to the Fae as the next in line to the throne, and his duty to his mate, who was a jaguar shifter and the Queen of the Jungle. She and her people's plight had won him over to Earth. They were the reason Father relented with the doorway in the Veil.

He comprehended as much as we did, our current situation needed to change. As much as he didn't want to risk us becoming targets because of our powers once again.

We followed the shore of the lake. The water lapped at the edges in a constant rhythm one could imagine as a heartbeat. Alongside the lake, trees rose into the sky and the many branches created thick shadows underneath making it appear cooler under the shade. The warm sun beat down on our heads and glinted off Patrick's and Declan's swords. I'd left my sword in my bed chambers. I loathed carrying the item I'd used to kill so many people. No matter how clean it was, I imagined it stained with blood. Up ahead, I spotted a narrow path through the forest. Patrick tried getting in front of me again. He couldn't seem to help himself, but I beat him to the path and walked along the dirt track. Branches from the nearby trees brushed against our shoulders and arms, releasing a tangy aroma of eucalyptus. Australia was an unusual country with its flora and fauna. I'd visited the place a few times, but I'd never ventured this deep into the forests.

Declan and Patrick were quiet beside me as they kept their focus on searching for threats.

The path weaved through the tall, slender trees. Birds fluttered from tree to tree letting out squawks of annoyance at our intrusion into their home territory. Thick fernery undergrowth reached waist height. Now and then a rustle came from underneath them as we disturbed more of the wildlife. The forest ended at a small clearing and the trees parted revealing a cabin nestled amongst the fauna like the owner had built it to blend in with its surroundings. A timber porch wrapped around the cabin. On the porch, a lover's seat hung from ropes and swung back and forth as Saoirse in her usual pretty pink dress crooned to the baby in her arms. The front door burst open so fast it slammed into the wall with a thud. A man stormed in front of Saoirse. His eyes glowed golden. Wild and ferocious, as though he'd rip us limb from limb if we moved another inch.

Patrick moved first, drawing his sword. The man growled so deeply the hairs on my arm stood on end. Saoirse took one glance at my face and jumped to her feet in a swirl of pink fabric. She placed the baby into the man's arms giving him no option but to hold him.

"Lorcan," she cried and raced across the short distance.

I ran toward her and caught her in my arms. Her arms wrapped around my neck in a stranglehold, making me cough.

"Sorry," she said, easing her tight grip. "I can't believe you're here at long last." She shoved me backward, then hauled me into her arms again.

I let her. She was my favorite sister. The one who'd always get up to mischief with me when we were youngsters. She was the closest to me in age, but it was her sassiness matching mine that made us so close.

The man cleared his throat.

"Arrow." She turned to the man. "This is Lorcan."

"So I gathered," he said, stepping closer and holding the baby protectively in his arms. "You should have waited before running off."

"I didn't run off." She placed her hands on her hips. "I promised I'd never leave you again."

"I know, sweetheart, but I meant for your protection."

"Lorcan would never hurt me." She folded her arms over her chest.

"She's right." I crossed my arms and matched her stance. "I'd never hurt her."

The man shuffled the baby into one arm and held out his hand. "Arrow Goldstein."

I clasped his hand and shook it. "Lorcan O'Cleirigh."

"Saoirse has told me a lot about you," Arrow said.

"All preposterous and untrue," I said.

Arrow's lips twitched. "I'm sure."

"Unless she told you how great I am, then in that case, it's true."

Saoirse laughed and threw her arm around my shoulder. "I've missed you."

"I've missed you too. Are you going to introduce me to the little prince?"

"He's a part wolf shifter," Arrow said.

"Aye, but all Fae prince," I said.

Saoirse held her arms out for the baby and Arrow placed him in her arms with a look of such love and affection it was easy to see the man loved them both. I was glad she'd found the type of love she'd longed for. The all-consuming love our parents had for each other. Fated mates were such a strong connection it was impossible to resist.

"This is Ailbhe." She tickled the baby under the chin.

The young prince giggled. His chubby cheeks glowed a rosy pink with health and happiness.

I dipped a bow. "A pleasure to meet you, Your Highness."

The baby laughed even more and held his arms out to me.

"I think he wants to say hello to his uncle," Saoirse said. "It'd be handy if Sophia was here."

I clasped the baby under his arms and lifted him across the small distance. "Why would Rian's mate help?"

"Didn't he mention since she's telepathic she can hear the thoughts of shifter young?"

"No, he didn't."

"I guess he had other things on his mind."

"Aye." I turned my attention to Ailbhe. "Well, little prince, what do you say? Should your favorite uncle show you the way of the Fae?"

The baby gurgled incoherent noises, but he was trying to tell me something. I nodded as though I understood him. His indigo-rimmed eyes were the same as all the royals. He was one of us.

"His Uncle Sledge will fight you for the favorite uncle title," Arrow said.

"He can have two favorite uncles. Can't you?" I gazed into the observant eyes of the baby. "One wolf shifter favorite uncle and one Fae favorite uncle. He'll need us for both sides of his powers."

"He will." Saoirse flung her arm around Arrow's waist and snuggled into his side. "How long are you here for and why have you brought guards with you?"

"It will depend on you how long I'm here for."

"In what way?"

"Father sent me here to convince you to come home."

"I am home." Her back straightened.

"To the Summer Court."

"Did he forget he imprisoned me? Then kicked me out?"

"No, he hasn't forgotten. He's recognized he was wrong to treat you so abysmally and he wants me to take you home so he can apologize."

Saoirse puffed out a breath through her clenched teeth. Arrow rubbed her back until some of the tension left her body.

After a long silence, she said, "I need to think about it."

"I wouldn't have expected anything less from you. So where am I staying?"

"You and your guards?" She peered at Patrick and Declan who stood a short distance away on alert to the surrounding forest searching for threats.

"Aye, they're part of Father's plan. He's opened a doorway in the Veil, but we must travel with guards for our protection." I rolled my eyes.

Saoirse giggled. "As if you need protecting."

"I keep saying the same thing."

"Honey," Arrow said. "We don't have enough room for them all here. They'll have to stay with Sledge at his hotel."

I stared at the cabin behind them. It appeared large enough for a family, but having Fae guards as well would put most people off having them stay in their house.

"I get to meet Briana's mate too?"

Saoirse nodded while biting her lip.

"I can't wait, but first, can we talk for a while like we used to?"

"Of course," Saoirse said. "Arrow how about you head to Sledge's place with the baby while Lorcan and I catch up?"

Arrow scowled. "I don't enjoy leaving you alone."

Saoirse kissed his cheek. "I won't be alone. My brother and two Fae guards are here with me."

"Fine," Arrow said and held his arms out for the baby. I handed him over. "I'll see you later, little prince."

Arrow kissed Saoirse then walked toward a truck and placed the baby inside before climbing into the vehicle and driving away sending up a cloud of red dust in his wake.

"He's very protective. Is it a wolf trait or is something wrong here?"

"It's a wolf trait, but we have had a little trouble."

My head snapped in her direction. "What trouble?"

"Nothing like what you're thinking," she said. "There's a female wolf shifter who has been causing trouble, but she's locked in the prison now. She can't do anything from there."

I pressed my lips together. The problem with trouble was it sneaked up on you when you least expected it. Like the Trappers. Was this woman a bigger threat than Saoirse believed? Was her life in danger being here?

It was a good thing I'd come when I did.

I'd protect my sister and her baby.

Nothing and no one would hurt our family ever again.

CHAPTER FOUR
PEPPER

FLYING ON A BROOMSTICK would have been preferable to the flight I'd had on the airplane. Hours upon hours of a rude couple sitting beside me. Then there was the air steward who'd refused to serve me more than two alcoholic drinks on a nineteen-hour flight. A ridiculous rule which I'm sure she made up to spite me. Few people accepted the way I dressed. Apart from those who hired me, they had no right to say anything even if they wanted to. Some had, but they'd soon learned the errors behind their ways when I'd left them high and dry without my help.

Never get on a witch's bad side. We have a long memory of those who treated us poorly.

I paid the taxi driver well for his long drive from the airport to Crystal Creek. He hadn't wanted to travel the distance at first but once I'd flashed a wad of cash in front of his eyes, he'd agreed.

Money always made a difference. It was why we coveted it so.

The quaint town he drove through was full of old buildings that intrigued me. I'd visited Crystal Creek before, but they'd been fleeting visits where I'd performed my magic and left. The tarred streets were clean. Not one piece of litter flew in the breeze rustling the trees lining the streets. People strolled the shop fronts casually as though they had all the time in the world to enjoy the sunny day. The taxi pulled up at a large white homestead. I paid him quickly since the spell I'd placed around the town would make it uncomfortable for him to stay inside too long.

I stepped out and watched him speed away as though he was leaving the Munster's mansion with monsters and ominous black clouds overhead. Instead, a large, white, homely looking two-story homestead with a wrap-around verandah stood before me. Many windows lined the building's façade. So many rooms in one building. The exterior was pretty in an understated way. Picturesque was the word that sprang to my mind. The building gave the impression of being as old and as pleasant as the town. In the front garden, flowers bloomed, adding appeal to step inside the premises. I opened the white metal gate expecting it to creak like mine did back home, but it didn't, it was as well cared for as the rest of the town. A nervousness overtook me as I walked up the stairs to the front door. I knocked on the solid timber wood, sensing the vibrations from the supernatural creatures inside. One perk of being a witch. We sensed magic and by the power coming through the door, there were a lot of supernatural creatures inside or there was one enormously powerful being like a King or Queen.

My hand buzzed with the power and the excitement to find out.

The door swung open, and Sledge stood in the doorway looking his usual larger-than-life self. The man who was a distant cousin smiled in greeting even though he appeared tense by the lines around his eyes.

"Pepper, come in." He waved me inside.

I flung my cape behind me and stepped over the threshold. The entrance way held a hallstand with coats hanging from the hooks. A potted plant reached toward the sunlight streaming in through the glass panel next to the door. From further inside the building, the power intensified, and it wasn't from the Alpha wolf beside me who appeared happier than I'd ever seen him, which could only account for one thing. He'd claimed his fated mate.

"I see you've embraced your destiny," I said.

He tilted his head and studied me with his blue eyes. "Always so observant, aren't you?"

"I have to be in my line of work." I placed my one piece of luggage on the timber floor. A large square vintage case made in the toughest of brown leather. Lighter tan leather straps held the sides together. Inside one side contained my clothes, and on the other was a set of drawers that stored all the essentials to make potions. "What do you need?"

"Straight to the point as always." His lips firmed. "Come inside and we'll talk more."

He lifted my case with ease even though it contained many glass vials and apparatus, which had been hell to get through customs. That, along with the ones strapped to my body in the pouch at my waist, but I had a spell for just about anything I needed. Including one that let customs officials overlook my strange baggage contents.

I followed Sledge along the hallway. He paused at a door, opened it, and placed my case in the room, then shut the door. I raised my eyebrows in question, but he kept walking into the large kitchen where an assortment of supernatural creatures sat at the table. My gaze scanned them all then stopped on one in particular. Striking blue eyes blazed back at me. A rim of pure indigo swirled into a bright flare drawing me in even deeper to the swirling depths of his gaze. His full lips pulled into an arrogant smirk, but it suited him. My body stirred in places that weren't appropriate. On top of his head, a crown of thorns stirred to life ruffling his silvery-blond hair. A Fae prince. Why was I surprised? I forced my gaze to the person beside him even though I hungered to keep learning every detail on his too-handsome face. Another Fae, Princess Briana sat next to him. Sledge stepped behind her and rubbed her shoulders affectionately. She gazed up at her mate with such love a lump formed in my throat.

"You remember my mate, Briana," Sledge said.

"Yes, the Fae princess. You've accepted your fate?"

"Aye," Briana said. "Sledge won me over."

I snorted. "He has a habit of winning people over."

"In what way?" she asked.

I ignored her question and turned to the others deliberately not looking at the Fae prince. Had the others noticed me staring at him? Had my mouth fallen open as I'd gazed at his beauty with awe?

"I've met Arrow, and I assume the baby and woman are yours?"

"Yes, she's Briana's sister, Saoirse," Sledge said.

Saoirse looked in my direction, but she said nothing. My gaze snapped back to the Fae prince on its own accord. He glowered in my direction. He was so similar in looks and coloring to the two Fae women that he had to be their brother, but I'd learned to never jump to conclusions. Facts kept me alive.

"And he is?" I asked Sledge since the Fae prince hadn't stopped glaring at me with that smirk on his face. The tense muscles in his shoulders appeared he was more ready to attack me rather than speak to me.

"Their brother, Lorcan," Sledge said.

"Three Fae royals. Quite the gathering. Who wants to tell me why you summoned me here for this meeting?"

The hostility coming from the prince was as powerful a vibration as the pure magic humming from their bodies. It didn't detract from the allure of his pretty face though. How stupid to think he was good-looking? Of course he was. All Fae were from what I'd seen of the Fae royals.

"Have a seat. You had a long flight."

"I'll stand, thanks." I backed toward the doorway, so I had a quick escape if I needed it. If the Fae wanted to overpower me, they'd be able to do it with ease before

I even yanked out a potion and threw it at them. Not that I wanted to, but there were times I'd needed to use potions to flee dangerous situations. I didn't imagine Sledge would bring me into his home to attack me, but looking after myself was what I was used to.

"Would you like a cup of tea?" Briana asked, standing.

I peered around the room, seeing every eye on me. "Sure."

Whatever was going on here, I didn't want to be here. I should have listened to my dreams.

Briana moved to the kettle and set it on the stove. She busied herself at the counter fetching cups from the cupboard enough for everyone by the looks of it. Silence filled the kitchen as shrewd glances passed from one person to the next. The sound of the water bubbling and then the kettle whistling was the single noise in the room to break the tension. Briana poured the water into the cups. Sledge walked over to his mate and helped carry them to the table. He stepped over to me last and handed me the cup with a small smile.

"Sorry to bring you into this," he said.

"You don't seem too sorry since you've been hounding me for weeks."

"It's important."

I blew across the steaming liquid. "It always is."

He returned to the table and sat beside Briana, who'd reclaimed her seat. There was one empty chair left beside the Fae prince, but I didn't care for sitting beside him even if he was the most attractive man in the room and made me think of a star-lit night, sensual touches, and sex. Eyes the color of crushed amethyst and sapphire gems glared at me.

What was his problem?

I understood he might have an issue since it was the magic of witches which had helped the Trappers capture the Fae and led to their deaths. Did he know the Trappers had forced most of those witches to work with them if they didn't agree to the pay? Sure, some had traded our wares for a price during the incident too, but this was the way we always worked. It wasn't our fault if the humans had used our potions for evil. We didn't police our products once they left us. If we did, then no one would come to us. We'd be useless. Powerless. At least we held a fraction of power in our mortal bodies.

Perhaps that was another of his problems. Maybe he didn't like mortals. Whatever. If he didn't stop glaring at me, then I'd slip a potion into his tea and turn him into a frog or something likewise appalling to a Fae prince. But why did he have to be so good-looking? It would have been easier if he wasn't. And why did he make me want to have sex with him when I didn't even know him?

His lips twitched into a sensual smirk as though he read my mind. If only I could wipe that smirk off his face by sitting on it. I lifted the cup to my lips and drank the tea so I wouldn't mutter a spell. Either to stop me lusting after him or one where I could sate my lust. The conflicting emotions were churning in my mind.

"Since you helped with my dad, then I'm sure you can guess we need an upgrade on the barrier you've created for the town," Sledge said, snapping me back to the problem I was here for.

"What sort of upgrade?"

Sledge rolled his massive shoulders. "We found the culprit who attacked Dad, but we think she wasn't working alone. She's a wolf shifter sent here from England."

"That's not much information to go on. The town has a protection spell to send humans away. I can't upgrade the spell to include wolf shifters otherwise you won't be able to get in."

The Fae prince stood, drawing my gaze to the width of his shoulders, the way his clothes clung to his chest, down to his waist but then the table blocked the rest from my view. Probably a good thing.

"If this place isn't safe, we should all return to the Summer Court," he said.

"You sound like Father," Saoirse said.

Lorcan narrowed his eyes. "Think of the young prince in your arms if you won't think about your safety."

Saoirse passed the baby to Arrow and then stood. Her hands glowed with her magic.

"Don't tell me I'm not protecting my son."

Lorcan blanched. "I didn't mean it that way. Sorry, Saoirse. I understood more than anyone you'd be the best mother ever."

"Damn right," Arrow muttered.

"Ugh, family," I murmured. The scene had cooled the instant lust burning through my limbs.

Lorcan's startling eyes snapped toward my face. His glare tempted me to flip him the finger, but he glanced away fast and sat back in his chair.

"What do you suggest?" Sledge asked. "I need to protect the town and my new family members."

Right. Sledge was now a part of the Fae royal family. What a turn of events. I churned the options over in my mind and paced across the doorway. If the other person trying to take over Crystal Creek was a wolf shifter, then I wouldn't be able to place a protection spell for their species. For what other creature would try to take over a wolf shifter town? If it was someone else, then in theory, I could single out a species in separate potions but there were too many to consider. If I made a spell for all of them, I'd be here for months and if the person attacked again before I'd protected against the species who was a threat, then all my work would be pointless. Besides, it was probably another wolf shifter.

"Well?" Lorcan snapped.

"I'm thinking." I shot a glare in his direction.

"What if..." I shook my head. "No that wouldn't work."

I paced over to the window and stared outside, giving my back to the group so I could think without seeing them staring at me. The Australian forest full of gum trees and wattle bushes surrounded Crystal Creek. There were lots of places a person might hide and plan an attack. Two figures dressed in bright red paced around the side of the house. The men had swords strapped to their backs. Such an unusual sight to see.

"You have guards patrolling the house?"

"I do," Lorcan said.

His voice traveled over the nape of my neck to my ears sending a ripple of pleasure from the warmth of his breath on my skin. Since when did he sneak up behind me? He was so close now, the heat from his body radiated toward mine and I liked it as much as I'd thought I would. I spun around. His body was inches from mine. So close that if I swayed toward him, I'd be able to press my front to his front. I dropped my gaze taking in the sight of his solid legs that were previously hidden beneath the table. His scent made my head swim with more images of us in bed, hot and sweaty with sex. I swallowed the moisture building in my mouth. Someone sneezed, and I remembered we weren't alone. I stepped around him taking the empty seat at the table now he was no longer sitting. My legs were quivering as though he'd almost brought me to orgasm. I brushed my hair back from my face and took a deep, cleansing breath.

"In all honesty, there isn't anything I can do for more protection. There are too many species to create a spell for each one and surely the person she was working with is a wolf shifter?"

Sledge nodded his head as though he'd expected my answer.

His downfallen expression made me blurt out, "I have another solution." My lips twitched into a smirk. "I'll make a truth potion for your prisoner, then we can question her."

"Good idea," Arrow said. "She hasn't given us any information so far."

"You won't be going near her," Saoirse said.

"Who will have Sledge's back if not me?" Arrow asked. "I'm his best friend."

"I don't want Sledge talking to Eloise either," Briana grumbled under her breath.

"Lorcan can," Saoirse said. "Won't you?"

Lorcan strode back to the table and patted his sister on the head affectionately. "For you, anything."

She reached up and swatted his hand away. "Don't mess my crown."

Her brother had ruffled not one flower in her princess crown during his antics but why would he mess with the perfection of the flowers? Power hummed from her crown in the same way as all their crowns hummed. So much magic in one room made me giddy. That had to be the reason I was reacting so sexually attracted to the prince. If not that, then I needed to get out of here before I embarrassed myself.

"If you don't mind, I need to find a place to stay for tonight. I can come back tomorrow," I said.

"You can stay here. There's plenty of room. It's a hotel," Sledge said with a teasing glint in his blue eyes.

"Don't expect me to pay you. This is on your dime."

Sledge laughed. "I wouldn't dream of it."

"I assume the room you put my bag in is mine."

"Yep. It was the one Briana stayed in before she came to her stubborn senses and became my mate."

"I'm not stubborn," Briana said indignantly.

Saoirse and Lorcan laughed. His happiness did things to my insides that I didn't want to examine.

I left the room. Happy families weren't my thing. My extended family wasn't close, and we didn't stay in touch. I wasn't sure if it said more about me or them.

CHAPTER FIVE

LORCAN

P EPPER.

A witch.

How had I felt attracted to her the instant she walked into the room? She was gorgeous. Sultry gray eyes that reminded me of a stormy sky. Thick lips that I longed to plunder with my own or better yet, have her on her knees with my aching cock in her mouth. I'd wrap my fingers in her thick dark hair and lose myself in the pleasures she promised with the heated looks she'd thrown my way. She was thinking of me the same way. I was certain of it. But taking a witch of all women to bed would make me depraved.

The witch's black cloak flowed behind her like a dark cloud of smoke. She reminded me of another witch from another time. The last time I'd seen Saltine, Trappers had attacked and left her surrounded by the ruins of the cottage. Her visions had prepared her for the Fae King's and my visit that night. She'd produced the potion for me to sense any Trapper and their location. Saltine had another potion requiring only one drop to make us immune to other witches' powers while we went on our hunt.

She'd also tasked me with keeping her greatest treasure safe.

We'd left her on the cusp of death amongst her ruins as she requested, mind you. We would have sought help for our witch seer if she'd allowed us.

Pepper was beautiful. Her dark hair hung over the thickness of her hooded cloak in such a way the strands blended into the material except for the long red streak hanging to her waist. What was she hiding under the cloak? Besides a body I hungered to see naked. She hadn't removed it, which was poor manners in my eyes. I dragged my thoughts from the woman I shouldn't desire to the matters I should focus on.

"What aren't you all telling me?" I asked.

"The prisoner, Eloise, sought to steal Arrow from me," Saoirse said. "I put her in her place."

"She's lucky you didn't kill her," I said.

"She was but perhaps it would have been better for Sledge and Briana if I had." Saoirse frowned.

Briana held up her hand to stop me from asking questions. "Eloise attacked Sledge's father and almost killed him because she wanted Sledge for herself."

"Who is this woman? Where did she come from?"

"She's a female wolf shifter we exchanged with a pack in England. Our male numbers are greater in Australia while England's numbers of wolf shifters favor females," Sledge said. "It's something my dad organized."

"I can't wait to be a part of the interrogation."

"You can't kill her," Saoirse said.

I smirked.

"I'm serious, Lorcan."

"Relax," I said, but I wouldn't agree to not kill her. She'd hurt two of my sisters. Harming my family deserved punishment in my eyes. "Can we trust the witch?"

Changing the subject was the best course of action right now. Plus, I hungered to know more about Pepper. Who was she? What did she want? Could I scratch the instant lust she'd invoked in my body?

My sisters shrugged. They were as hesitant about witches as me. Understandable given our history.

"She helped me," Arrow said. "I suppose she did it for payment, but she could have left me encased in ice."

I rose an eyebrow. "How did you become an icicle?"

"Father." Saoirse firmed her lips.

"Right," I said, recalling the tale she'd told me about Father finding her on Earth with the wolf shifter and going a little crazy.

"I trust Pepper," Sledge said. "She might want payment for her services but why shouldn't she get paid for spells and potions?"

I rolled my shoulders. He was right, but witches were powerful. If their spells and potions fell into the wrong hands, then we'd be in trouble like before.

"We need to get this little guy home to bed," Saoirse said, standing with the baby on her hip.

Arrow stood and hoisted the baby into his hold. Ailbhe held his arms toward Sledge, who stood and reached across the table for his nephew. The baby gurgled happily while Sledge carried him to the front door. Saoirse kissed my cheeks and hurried after them.

"So," I said, staring at Briana. "When are you telling Father about your fated mate?"

Her shoulders sagged. "Do you think he's ready to hear it?"

I tilted my head and studied her. She appeared so much happier than she had before she met Sledge. Her mate had lifted the darkness from her. Father would see the happiness shining from her and be thankful.

"Yes. He wants us to be happy. You look happy."

"I'm scared to tell him after the way he reacted with Saoirse."

I reached across the table and clasped her hand. "He was wrong, and he sees the error of his reaction. I'm not sure why he snapped as he did with Saoirse, but he's back to his old self now."

Briana brushed a hand across her eyes as though she was brushing away tears, but not a single drop fell onto her cheeks.

"I'll tell him when you convince Saoirse to return home."

I laughed. "Stop putting off the inevitable. You don't want to end up like Rian hiding the fact he had a mate for ten years. Secrecy and distance will take a toll on any relationship."

"Have you had word from Rian of late?"

"Aye. He's well in the Amazon jungle surrounded by a Fae army, a jaguar army, and mated to the Queen of the Jungle. Nothing or no one will harm him. It's you and Saoirse I'm worried about. The occurrences here leave a lot to be concerned about."

"They do." She frowned. "You don't..."

"No, I don't sense any Trappers."

"Good." Her breath eased out of her lungs in a way that made it seem she'd been tense the entire time until my admission.

I squeezed her hand. "We killed them all. If there was one drop of Trapper blood in existence, then I'd sense it."

"What are you two talking about?" Sledge asked, walking back into the room.

"Nothing important," Briana said, sliding her hand out from under mine.

I laughed at Briana always trying to disguise her pain. "We were talking about her telling Father about you."

"I'm ready whenever you are, sweetheart."

They stared at each other having a silent conversation with their eyes. The intimacy between them reminded me of Mother and Father. Fated mates were worth waiting for. No matter the length of time. I might have been trying to fool everyone into thinking I'd choose a mate, but there wasn't a chance I'd settle for anything less than my fated mate. I'd always assumed they'd be

Fae but with my brother mated to a jaguar shifter and two sisters mated to wolf shifters, then it might be any supernatural species. Above all, now we possessed the opportunity to travel back to Earth.

I rose from my chair. "I'll leave you two to talk. Which room is mine?"

"I'll show you," Sledge said.

I fixed Briana with a stare. "You should return to the Summer Court then come back through the doorway Father created."

"Why?"

"Then you'll have guards accompany you. By the sound of things around here, extra protection wouldn't go astray."

Briana's eyes glittered with defiance and the need to say a rebuttal hovered on her pursed lips, but she nodded her head instead.

Sledge led the way from the kitchen and along the hallway.

"I'm surprised she agreed," Sledge said in a low voice. "She's so stubborn."

"Aye," I said. "Briana knows I'm right though."

Sledge laughed. "Even then she's more often than not set in her way, but I love her even more for it."

My lips twitched. Of course, fate would send Briana a mate who loved her stubbornness.

"Here we are." Sledge stopped outside a door. "You didn't bring any luggage?"

"No. I'd hoped Saoirse would head home and set everyone's minds at ease."

"You didn't count on her being as stubborn as Briana?" His eyebrow lifted in question.

I gave him a wry smile. "I should have known better."

Sledge slapped me on the shoulder. "I have a sister. I can't imagine what having five is like."

"They're wonderful and infuriating but don't tell them I said that."

Sledge ran his fingers over his lips. "Your secret is safe with me."

I opened the door and peered inside. "Thanks for the accommodation."

"No problem. I'll show your guards to their rooms, too. Their pacing outside is annoying. Don't they realize I'd hear anything coming?"

"Probably not," I said. "It's been a long time since they were amongst other supernatural creatures. Perhaps they've forgotten the skills of a wolf shifter."

Sledge cracked his knuckles. "I'll remind them."

I laughed. "Be prepared. They are guards."

He rolled his shoulders. "They might be guards but they're in my territory. I think they'll need more training here if you're staying."

"With a bit of luck, Saoirse will relent sooner rather than later before you and my guards hurt each other." I grinned. "Although, I wouldn't mind testing my skills on fighters other than Fae."

"Oh, bring it, brother-in-law," Sledge teased. "Saoirse trained me how to use a sword and Briana trained me with her staff."

"Well, then this will be a fun trip to Earth."

Sledge walked back to the kitchen chuckling.

I stepped into the room and closed the door. A sumptuous-looking bed was the centerpiece of the bedroom. Multiple pillows and plush blankets in earthy tones invited me to lay my weary head. On the wall behind the headboard was a large forest painting bringing the outside in. From the ceiling hung golden lights giving the room a soothing atmosphere. To the left was a set of glass doors opening to the garden beyond. The moon shone through the glass with a twinkle drawing my gaze to admire the beauty of Earth.

The Summer Court nights were even more exquisite but seeing the difference in the realms made each one even more special. A yellow light flared to life on the ground. Then another and another. I recognized the flicker of candles. I walked to the door. Whatever was going on outside, I didn't like it. Unease coated my skin making goose bumps form as though I was cold, and Fae didn't feel the cold.

As I opened the door, a shadow flitted around the candles like a dark butterfly of the night. Soft chanting drifted across the air. Her voice was even more alluring than it had been earlier. Husky and sensual notes slid across my skin turning the goose bumps into a pleasant sensation. I shouldn't want her. Shoving the desire to the back, I skulked closer to the witch. Drawn to her in a way I didn't understand apart from the sexual appeal. That part was easy. She sat on the ground and drew her cloak around herself. What was she up to?

"I sense you, Lorcan," the witch's voice echoed across the night air as though there was more than one of her. Or she was a long way away when in fact she was so close I caught the soft fullness of her lips in the candlelight.

Why was I staring at her lips again? Imagining her taking me in her mouth and making me come undone beneath the light of the moon. What magic had the witch weaved over me?

CHAPTER SIX
PEPPER

THE FAE PRINCE'S HOSTILITY was like needles in my skin. It prickled and burned. Made me uncomfortable. But underneath I could have sworn I sensed his interest in me as a woman. His conflicting emotions didn't dampen the way my body responded to his presence. A tingle of awareness circled my stomach.

I wasn't doing anything wrong, but every second in his presence made me consider I was. He edged closer to me, and the pin-prick sensation intensified, but underneath there was still the lure of him as a man. I sure didn't understand how I could want him with the mindless passion trying to force its way to the front of my body. The candles flickered as though a breeze blew across them, but Lorcan stepped into the circle opposite me, and the candles settled. My spell wasn't complete and if I broke my position, then I'd have to start all over again.

His indigo and blue eyes peered down at me with obvious unease glittering in their fathomless depths.

What did I ever do to make him distrust me? Nothing. We'd never met before today, so he had no reason to despise me. I'd only met Fae through Sledge.

"What is your problem with me?" I asked.

Lorcan's head jerked back as though I'd shocked him with my outright question.

"What are you doing?" He pointed at the candles and the small pouches beside them.

Arrogant jerk not answering my question and asking one of his own.

"What does it look like I'm doing?" I threw it back since I was just as arrogant as him.

"Spell casting."

"Correct."

A silence descended between us, and it wasn't comfortable with the tension between us. I didn't imagine the sexual tension or the animosity coming from him. It was a heady combination that my body appeared to like if the way my nipples pebbled under my clothes was any indication. We stared, sizing the other up. He was too good-looking not to stare at. The moonlight glinted off the angles of his face making him seem like a moon god chose him as his champion. I'd like to choose him to quench this insane lust running in waves through my body whenever he was near. Why did I want to take him to bed while he infuriated me? We both glanced away at the same time.

He squatted, drawing my gaze back in his direction. The thick muscles of his thighs bunched in my line of sight. They made my thighs quiver in response as though every move he made produced an equal reaction in my body. If he touched me, then what would happen?

"Will I get an answer if I ask what spell?" he asked in a deep voice that sent another wave of desire through my body.

I tilted my chin up. "What's it matter to you? I'm not hurting anyone."

"If you don't tell me what spell you're using, then I'll assume you're up to something sinister."

Were all Fae like this so arrogant and untrusting?

"If you must know, it's a protection spell."

"I figured as much," he muttered, poking a finger at one pouch containing a special mix of herbs. "What sort?"

"One to keep me safe while I sleep." I fixed him with a pointed glare.

How did he understand what a protection spell looked like?

Before I asked, he said, "I'll keep you safe."

"You?" I snorted. "I hardly think by the hostility rolling off you, you'd keep me safe."

He lowered himself to the ground and stretched out his long legs on either side of the candles. His feet came past me and for some bizarre reason, I experienced a sensation of being safer.

"I may not like witches, but I'd harm no one without due cause."

"And what would constitute due cause?"

"If anyone harmed my family or my people." He picked up one pouch and held it over the candle.

How did he realize I was about to burn the pouch? Smoke billowed from the herbs and drifted up into the dark sky. The aroma of garden sage, rosemary, rose, and mint filled the air between us. Lorcan drew in a deep breath as though the spell would protect him too. What did a powerful Fae Prince need protection from?

"Rest assured, I've harmed no one."

His eyes darkened as shadows passed over his face. He dropped the pouch into the center of the candles and the last remnants burned to nothing but smoke and ash.

"You have though, haven't you?"

He scowled. "I don't wish to talk about it."

"I suppose not." Leaning forward, I blew out the candles. The spell was complete, and I'd protected Sledge's hotel with the best spell.

The last scent of the herbs blew away on a sudden uplift in the breeze. An icy shiver ran along my neck and down my back.

"How are you cold wearing a cloak?" he asked.

I tugged the edges of the cloak around my shoulders then lifted the hood on top of my head.

"The material isn't thick."

"Seems an oversight on your seamstress's part."

I laughed. "My seamstress? I made the cloak myself after studying under a witch in Paris. All witches do."

With each stitch, we embedded a fraction of magic inside the cloak. It was supposed to add a layer of protection to our mortal bodies. We were lucky it worked a fraction, and we never grew sick, but we aged, albeit a lot slower than humans, but we wouldn't live forever like a Fae or wolf shifter.

His hand snapped out to the edge of the cloak hanging over my legs and he rubbed the material between his fingers.

"Why didn't you make it from thicker material?"

I yanked the cloak from his grasp. "We choose whatever speaks to us."

"Perhaps you weren't listening well then?" He cocked an eyebrow.

I collected the candles and stood. How dare he say I hadn't tuned into my gifts? I glared, but he stared back with an amused smirk on his too-handsome face. It made me want to wipe it off with my lips just to see him startled and less sure of himself.

"I listened."

"Perhaps," he said, running his gaze from my face down the length of my body. "Why aren't you listening to yourself now?"

"What do you mean?" I huffed.

He rose to his impressive height looking even more regal, refined, and in control. All the things I wasn't.

"You do." He lifted a hand and pushed the hood from my head. "You want to kiss me."

My heart pounded like an elephant's footfalls inside my chest. How did he understand what I'd been thinking?

"I do not," I spluttered.

"Shall we go inside, and I say the same thing in front of Sledge so he can confirm your lies?"

I narrowed my eyes. "I wouldn't want to kiss you if you were the last man I'd ever have the chance to kiss."

"No?"

"No."

"We'll see." He turned and walked back toward the open French doors in the room next to mine with the same open doors.

I stared at his cocky swagger way too long to deny Lorcan set my hormones racing and admit he was right. I wanted to kiss him. Have sex with him. Let him take me to the heights of pleasure and make me fall over the edge into bliss. But it was more. I longed to belong to someone. Be important for something other than my potions and spells. I lifted my hood back on my head. For a moment I'd imagined he'd kiss me even though I'd denied I wanted his kiss. He didn't though. Lorcan might be arrogant. Conceited. And alluring as all the Fae were, but he appeared to have morals too. We couldn't say the same for humans. I blinked fast to stop myself from crying.

I never cried.

Ever.

One intimate moment with a Fae Prince and I was ready to spill tears. What was up with that?

I fled to the relative safety of my bedroom and locked the French glass doors. The moon shone down on the patch where we'd sat as though marking the place as special. My gaze lifted to the night sky. Stars twinkled in the distance as though dancing across the darkness. When I died, would I become a star in the sky? It was an enchanting concept I'd held onto my entire life. One fueled by the tales my grandmother had told us about the gods living amongst the stars.

My fingers toyed with the edges of the thick red curtains, but I left them open. There was magical power in the moonbeams streaming into the room. I walked into the bathroom and undressed to a singlet and panties. The cold might bother me, but I preferred sleeping with as little on as possible. When I was at home, I slept naked.

I climbed the few steps to the platform bed and burrowed under the covers. Before too long, the lure of sleep drew me into the depths of a nightmare.

The moon disappeared behind the long fingers of a black hand. The hand crept closer to my face. My body wouldn't move though. Every muscle in my body froze in place. No limb would twitch, or joint would bend. I attempted to open my mouth and call for help, but it was like someone had sewn my lips shut. Yet the hand crept closer still until all I saw were the long taloned fingers and the thick palm descending toward my throat.

I blinked, and the hand vanished.

Red flames flickered in its place.

A fire roared toward me. The heat was so intense it felt like my flesh was melting from my body. This time when I tried to move I could. I ran, but I was in a fire ball. Flames bared down on me from all sides. It didn't matter which way I ran for it would engulf me in the orange heat. I screamed in vain for no one was around. They'd all escaped the fire but me.

As the flames closed in on me a hand clasped mine. Strong fingers were aglow with blue-green flames. I strained to tug myself free certain this person would burn me alive, but while the surrounding fire heated to an inferno, the hand on fire clasping mine was cool to the touch.

"Wake up, Pepper."

My shoulders shook not from fear but from the force of a pair of powerful hands.

As I struggled back to consciousness, I sat up and stared into the worried eyes of Lorcan.

"What?" I whispered through a throat that suffered as if the fire had stripped every ounce of moisture from my body. As though I'd been in the flames about to die.

"You were dreaming." He released one shoulder to brush the hair back from my sweaty face.

Tingles danced their way across my skin and radiated across my scalp.

Another nightmare. The same one I'd had these past few months. Whenever I was near Crystal Creek, they came with more frequency than when I was elsewhere. It was why I hadn't wanted to return here.

Lorcan's touch continued, as though he wanted to keep soothing me for all time. I tilted my head into his palm on the next caress of his hand. The power of the Fae royal thrummed through his palms, but he kept the magic under control.

"Want to tell me about it?" he asked, cupping my cheek in his palm.

"Just a nightmare," I whispered, blinking at the allure of his strangely colored eyes.

If I crossed the small distance and planted my lips on his, would it chase the nightmare away? Would he allow me such a pleasure? My body tingled and pulsed with the need to do that. As soon as Lorcan was near, my body flooded with desire. And he was near. I was in bed. He was sitting on my bed. With me. It wouldn't take much to admit I wanted to kiss him. Have sex with him.

"Some nightmare," he murmured. "I swear I smelled smoke."

All thoughts of sex vanished, and I jerked out of his touch and stood. No. It wasn't possible. It was a nightmare.

A knock thudded on the door. I strode over to it and yanked it open.

"What?" I snapped.

"Everything all right in here?" Sledge asked, peering over my shoulder and glancing around the room. His gaze stopped on Lorcan. "I heard you scream."

"I had a bad dream. Lorcan woke me."

Sledge frowned. "Why can I smell fire?"

"No fire." I waved my hand inside the room. "Maybe it was my candles."

Even though every candle in the room was unlit.

"Now, if you'll both leave so I can go back to sleep." I pointed at the door so Lorcan would get the hint.

He rose and walked toward Sledge but not before sweeping his gaze over my body. Heat lit up inside me like he'd touched my bare skin. Crap. I was in a singlet and panties. At least I wasn't naked. I kept my chin high until he stepped through the door. Then I slammed the door shut and sagged against it.

It wasn't real.

The nightmare was exactly that. A nightmare.

Yet, the nagging suspicion I was the same as my great, great many times grandmother wouldn't leave me. I ran to my pouch and grabbed the amulet inside. The round metal object engraved with intricate knots warmed to my touch. A few years ago, a witch at a flea market had sold it to me as a protection charm. I twirled the coin-sized amulet in my fingers and sunk to the ground, resting my chin on my drawn-up knees. Over and over, I spun the amulet hoping it would protect me from my dream because if I possessed the abilities like my relative, then the nightmare wasn't a figment of my imagination.

It was a premonition.

CHAPTER SEVEN
PEPPER

B LEARY-EYED, SINCE I'D GOT no more sleep, I walked
into the kitchen as the first stream of sunlight
streaked across the predawn sky. I placed a box
containing all my must-have herbs on the counter and
filled the kettle with water. Each movement came with
ease as I made a batch of tea to help see me through the
day and chase away my nightmare. I inhaled the scent
of the yarrow. The smell alone would bring clarity to my
cloudy mind, then I placed it in a small pot. Next, I added
chamomile and a dash of cinnamon to boost my energy.
I poured the boiling water into the pot and let it steep.

While waiting for the tea to brew, I lit a bunch of
rosemary leaves to chase away the last disturbances in
my mind from the nightmare.

"What's this stench?" Sledge asked, walking into the
kitchen, and waving a hand in front of his nose.

"You want me here, get used to it," I said, even
snappier than I usually was after my disturbing
nightmare.

Sledge frowned and opened the refrigerator. He pulled out a carton of milk, set it on the counter then made a cup of coffee with the hot water in the kettle. He sipped the mug and observed me.

"What?" I snapped.

"You seem extra standoffish this morning. Did something bad happen between you and Lorcan, because if it did, then I'll get rid of him."

Standoffish? Was that how I came across to others? I frowned and peered into the depths of the tea, then poured it into a cup.

"Nothing happened," I said.

Apart from me wanting to kiss him and him being aware of the fact. Also, where he woke me from my nightmare and saved me from watching myself burn to death like I'd witnessed other nights in the dream.

"Are you sure? He was in your room, and you screamed."

"I had a nightmare, and he woke me," I said, lifting the cup to my lips, I sipped the tea. "What's with the overprotective act?"

"It's not an act, Pepper. You are family. Wolves protect their family."

I snorted. "Mine doesn't."

He leaned his hip against the counter. "What do you mean?"

"You forget, for the most part, my side of the family are witches. We're not the same and we never will be. So, save your talk of the family protection for your own family."

Sledge's mouth opened but Lorcan walked into the room looking way too handsome and well-rested. My heart jumped a beat. Sledge's mouth snapped shut, and he studied Lorcan in a more calculating manner than he already had before today.

"Do you have any more of the tea, Pepper?" Lorcan asked.

Did he want to drink my tea? Since when was he so willing to accept my help?

"No," I said and finished the rest of my cup.

"Shame," he said. "I guess I'll make my own."

He stepped around me and sniffed the herbs I had arranged on the counter. After selecting chamomile and mint, he brewed his cup of tea. Each movement he made was so self-assured it made me wonder how a Fae Prince had learned so much about herbs.

"What's the plan today?" Lorcan asked.

Sledge snapped out of his staring at us. "Pepper will make a truth spell and we'll visit Eloise in the jail then we'll get the answers we need from her."

"If it doesn't work?" Lorcan asked.

"My spells always work," I said.

"I meant what if we don't get the answers we need to put an end to this threat?"

"Oh."

"We will," Sledge said, with authority.

It was easy to see him in his role as Alpha of the pack, but whatever he said, I wasn't a part of his pack. The small part of wolf-shifter blood in my bloodline was so diluted now it connected us by the barest of threads. His claiming me as a member of his family was far-fetched in my eyes, but the claim might come in useful one day.

"Get out of the kitchen and leave me to make the serum." I pointed at the door.

"But breakfast?" Sledge said.

"You'll have to get it somewhere else."

"Come on," Sledge said. "I suppose we'll head to Arrow's and Saoirse's house for breakfast."

"Good," Lorcan said. "I need to talk to Saoirse, anyway."

Right. He was here for his family, and he'd soon head back to the Summer Court. See, wanting to kiss the Fae Prince was a ridiculous notion, one that would get me nothing but a onetime thing. Was one night all he wanted? I narrowed my eyes at Lorcan's departing head. Did he think I was easy? A frivolous woman who would kiss anyone and not care.

Anger fueled my body. Irrational since I understood nothing about being a prince. Or anything about Lorcan.

Not that I wanted to.

No. I'd keep away from him as far as possible while living in the same place. The same hotel. Our bedrooms were next door to each other.

No matter how tempted I was to kiss the arrogance from his face. I rolled my eyes at myself. Maybe a fling with the Fae Prince would do me good? I'd see what it was like, so I'd never have to wonder. It'd been a long time since I'd dated anyone. My body agreed with the notion, but my mind was still undecided.

I picked up the yarrow root and inhaled again. With enormous care, I selected belladonna next. Too much and I'd kill the person, then we'd never get the answers to the threat surrounding Crystal Creek. It sounded like Eloise needed to die though. I eyed the belladonna and contemplated adding a lethal dose.

No. That would be too easy for the traitor. She'd almost killed Sledge's dad and while I didn't consider myself his family, Sledge had taken on the big brother protective role. A small part of my icy heart warmed at the way he'd wanted to protect me.

Then I remembered Lorcan's words saying he wanted to protect me too. Did he mean that in a brotherly way as Sledge did? Or was he as intrigued with me as I was with him?

Did he want to kiss me as much as I wanted to kiss him?

CHAPTER EIGHT
LORCAN

S LEDGE DROVE ME, PATRICK, and Declan, in his enormous truck to my sister's new home. The forest whizzed by in a blur of gray-green leaves and a variety of tree trunks ranging from brown to reddish-brown, and a silvery white. The effect on my eyes was a little disorientating. I peered over my shoulder at Patrick and Declan, who had a similar white-faced expression. This would be their first time driving in a motor vehicle and it wasn't a pleasant experience for them.

"Do you have to drive so fast?" I asked.

"Nope." Sledge grinned but didn't slow down.

My mind drifted back to Pepper. She'd surprised me with her protection spell on the hotel. I'd always understood witches did nothing unless they were being paid and Sledge had said nothing about her protecting his hotel. Had she discussed placing a protection spell on the hotel with him? Had she charged him a price for it too?

Then there was the tea this morning which she'd been unwilling to share. Why? What did she have in the tea that she didn't want me to have? Or was this another case of a witch not doing anything for free?

Pepper attracted me too. What was the reason for the way she lured me? She was nothing like the pale Fae women I bedded. She was dark. Intriguing. So much sass in her that I wondered what she'd be like in bed. As wild and dark as I imagined. I shifted on the seat and stared out of the windscreen before my thoughts made it obvious where they were heading to the observant wolf shifter beside me.

He probably scented my desire for Pepper.

I was glad the witch didn't seem to have the same skill even though she was part of Sledge's family. All I sensed from her was a witch. Sledge would be the best person to ask about Pepper but the way he'd side-eyed us this morning gave me the impression he might not be inclined to answer the questions. Plus, Patrick and Declan were in the back seat. What would they make of me asking personal questions about a witch?

How was I even interested in her after the way witches had helped in our destruction?

I ran a finger over my crown letting the sensation of the Fae power settle my conflicting emotions. Besides, I wasn't here for myself. I was here to bring my sister home. Sledge swerved around a corner on the dirt track throwing me into the door of the truck. I righted myself and rubbed my elbow. Sledge grinned and slid the truck to a stop in front of the log cabin. Patrick and Declan scrambled from the back seat and took in a deep lungful of air.

"Was that necessary?" I asked. "It was their first time in a vehicle."

"These guards of yours need to understand everything about the way Earth is now." He shrugged.

"You're right. If we're here for a while, do you have a member of your pack who can teach them how to drive?"

"Sure." Sledge opened his door and strode to the front door.

My new brother-in-law appeared to have a problem with me. I'd have to uncover why later. First, it was time to talk to Saoirse again. I followed him to the front door. It swung open and Arrow waved us inside the cozy interior.

Saoirse walked toward us and placed Ailbhe in my arms.

"Hey," Sledge said.

Saoirse patted Sledge's muscular arm. "Your turn next. Let Ailbhe get to know his other uncle."

"I suppose," Sledge grumbled. "Is breakfast ready?"

"Nice of you to invite yourself over," Arrow said with a teasing grin.

"It was here, or my parent's house and you cook better but don't tell my mom I said that whatever you do. She'd tear strips off me," Sledge said.

Everyone laughed, but I filed the piece of information away. Ailbhe cooed, and I turned my attention to the newest Fae royal.

"Hello, little prince. What have you been up to?"

Ailbhe gurgled back, but I didn't understand him. His chubby little hand wrapped around my finger. A brief spark of power zapped between us.

"Aye," I said. "That's how you tap into your Fae power."

Everyone whirled to face us. I let a fraction of my Fae power into the finger Ailbhe held. The tip glowed blue-green. Ailbhe giggled. His little hand glowed a rainbow of colors. I sucked in a shocked breath. So did Saoirse.

"Grandfather..." she gulped.

My gaze met her tear-filled eyes. "His powers were the same color."

"This is the first time he's shown them." She stepped closer and placed a hand on Ailbhe's back.

"He has the old king's power. A family legacy."

She pursed her lips.

"You need to take him to the Summer Court and talk to Father. He'll be able to instruct you best on how the young prince can control his powers like his father did."

"No."

"Saoirse, don't be so stubborn."

She took Ailbhe from my arms. The baby wailed. Our loss of connection dissolved the Fae power in his wee hand. Saoirse handed him to Sledge and Ailbhe stopped crying.

"Come on, little guy, let's get you breakfast," Sledge said taking Ailbhe into the kitchen.

"Sweetheart?" Arrow asked.

"Go with Sledge and Ailbhe," she said.

We waited until they were in the kitchen. They might be out of sight and if they were anyone else out of earshot, but the wolf shifters would hear everything we said to one other.

"I'm not being stubborn," she hissed.

"You are. You're just like Father."

"How dare you?"

"It's true though, isn't it?"

We glared at each other.

"And here I'd longed for the day you'd come and see me."

"Don't be like that, Saoirse. I'll always have your back. Who helped you escape from the cell?"

"You did." She gave me a small smile.

"Who started a fight with Father, so you had a chance to leave?"

"You did," she said.

"See," I said. "I'm not telling you to go back and stay. I can see you're happy here. Our makers never meant us to remain in one realm alone."

She brushed a shaking hand through her long silvery-blonde hair.

"We were so horrible to each other." She sniffed. "What if he doesn't forgive me?"

"He doesn't need to forgive you. You were fighting for your mate. He understands how important they are more than anyone else. Why do you think he locked us all in the Summer Court? Everything he's done, the good and the bad, has been for his mate."

Her eyes lit with understanding that wasn't there before.

"I understand the need to protect my mate," she admitted. "I'd kill anyone who hurt Arrow."

Sledge's chuckle reverberated from the kitchen. Damn wolf shifters eavesdropping.

"I'm sure he would say the same about you."

"Damn right," Arrow said loud enough we overheard him.

"See." I waved my hand in the direction of the kitchen.

"Father wants you to return to the Summer Court. Mother wants to meet her grandchild more than anything. Our sisters are eager to meet him too."

"Even Aislinn?" She cocked an eyebrow.

"I'm sure she does, even if she'll give him a dagger for a present."

Saoirse laughed. "She still hasn't changed?"

"No. I worry about her."

"Me too."

"Ever since that horrific night..." Saoirse trailed off.

The night had marked all of us differently. Our scars ran deep below the surface of our skin. Those closest to us appreciated the extent of the injury. The pain. Despair and depression.

"I know."

That night had inflicted a wound on my soul. One that would never mend. No matter how hard I aimed to fix the dark stain, it never went away.

Arrow walked out of the kitchen and gathered Saoirse into his arms. She sagged into his embrace and let him take the pain from her body. I sensed the connection as all Fae did between fated mates. It was why we longed for one of our own so much.

But I didn't want a mate.

If I did, then she'd see my memories when I placed the Fae mating mark on her chest. I'd never let that happen. Those dark memories were mine alone. No one deserved to see the horror. The death. The blood. The fire.

"Fine, we'll go to the Summer Court for a temporary visit," Saoirse said.

"Of course," I said. "We can plan to leave after I help Sledge with the interrogation later today."

I walked around them and joined Sledge in the kitchen and sat at the table. Once again, the wolf shifter surprised me by pushing a plate of blueberry muffins toward me. Blueberry was a Fae favorite. Perhaps Sledge didn't have as much of an issue with me as I first assumed. Unless he was feeding me a favored food because he was now happy I'd be returning to the Summer Court.

Either way, my time in Crystal Creek was ending. My mission had been short. Saoirse agreeing to return home seemed too easy. A sense of unease slithered down my spine but where was the sensation coming from?

CHAPTER NINE
PEPPER

T HE TRUTH SERUM WAS ready. They hadn't returned from their breakfast yet, which was odd since it was almost lunchtime. I hadn't told them the exact time to return, but I'd said I'd need a few hours to make the potion. The small vial taunted me. I didn't enjoy making a potion as strong as this one, but when it was for a wolf shifter instead of a human, then I had to add more ingredients to ensure they worked on her supernatural abilities.

Some creatures were harder to work with than others.

My parents comprehended that too well. They'd died when they'd accepted a request from an elf from the Spring Court. The coven hadn't cared in the least my parents died while selling their wares. I'd left the Coven of the Blue Moon the second we'd lit their funeral pyres. I hadn't stepped foot on the coven grounds no matter what since I never liked the High Priestess, Miss Margo Manning, and she'd been no fan of mine either. She'd gate kept most of the spell books, anyway. It's why I'd stolen one from the locked cupboard on the night I left. Families would pass on their grimoires, but my family lost our grimoire the night the Trappers wrought their mass genocide of the Fae. Whoever told those human Trappers burning Fae alive would release their powers to them had a lot to answer for.

The front door opened and closed. Footsteps echoed along the wooden floorboards until they reached the kitchen. Four men came into the room Sledge, Lorcan, and two other Fae. His guards I'd seen through the kitchen window by the looks of the swords strapped to them.

"About time," I said.

"You said you needed a few hours," Sledge said.

"Right." I gathered the potion bottle and slipped it into the pouch at my waist. "Let's go, then with any luck, I can head home."

Sledge didn't look impressed and Lorcan's mouth twisted into a weird line of disapproval. Why did they all have to judge me? The guards appeared unaffected by my words, but why would they affect them? I'd never met them.

"I'm Pepper," I said, nodding at the men.

Their faces blanked, but a flash passed through their eyes. Oh, they didn't like me either. Well, sod them all.

"This is Patrick and Declan," Lorcan said for the two Fae who kept their lips shut.

"Whatever." I yanked my cloak around me and tugged the hood into place then walked around them.

Sledge rushed forward and joined me at the door. "Forget them," he whispered.

Startled, I flicked my gaze to his face.

"You don't need their approval or respect."

I swallowed the thickening emotions in my throat.

"Of course not," I agreed, even though their attitude stung like a thousand insect bites on my skin.

We walked outside into a blistery breeze whipping across the town. Wolf shifters walked by and nodded at Sledge. Not one wolf shifter stared at me even though I sensed their unease about me being in their town. It was the life of a witch, and you'd think I'd be used to it by now, but I wasn't. I don't think I'd ever be unaffected no matter the hard exterior I portrayed.

My hood kept the wind from whipping my long hair about my face and I kept my chin down as I walked the streets with Sledge by my side and the three Fae at my back. I didn't like them behind me. At any moment one of those guards might draw his sword and stab me in the back if I gave them a good reason.

I counted my steps to keep myself from turning around as we walked along the pavement in front of various buildings. After a few streets, Sledge stopped outside a solid brick building that gave off a sense of being a fortress more than one of the pleasant buildings we'd passed.

"In here," he said.

I followed him into the dimly lit building as though the poor lighting added to the sense of doom. A pair of wolf shifters in police uniforms sat at desks inside. Stacks of paper lined their desks while they typed on computers. They both peered up at our sudden intrusion and jumped to their feet at the sight of Sledge.

"How's the prisoner?" Sledge asked.

"The same," said the guard with the nametag, Bron.

"Difficult as always." Sledge grimaced. "We're trying a truth serum on her. Can you bring her to the interrogation room in chains? I don't want to take any chances of her attacking Pepper."

And there went the small warmth in my heart again. Sledge cared about my welfare. He might be the only one though. Maybe he was more family than I'd given him credit for.

The guards hurried through a door and left us waiting in the reception area. I sat in a chair and crossed my legs, bouncing my foot as though in time with a song. There was no music though. Not even in my head. Nervous energy zinged through my limbs that I hadn't got the proportions right for the potion. As good as the grimoire I'd stolen was, it didn't hold the answers to everything I needed to make spells for supernatural creatures. I suspected only my family's grimoire would contain the knowledge I so desperately longed for.

Minutes ticked by, then the guards returned looking a little rumpled. Sledge cocked an eyebrow but said nothing.

"She's chained to the desk," Bron said.

"Thanks," Sledge said.

He led the way to the interrogation room down the long corridor of the building. Through the window beside the door, a woman sat in handcuffs chained to a desk. One I recognized. Why hadn't her name registered?

"I've met her," I said.

"You have?" Sledge asked. "When?"

"Her pack lived in the town next to my hometown."

"Your hometown is in England?" Sledge asked.

"Yes. I lived in Linton with my parents and her pack ran the Bray Forest. I wasn't friends with her or anything, but I have seen her around."

"Would she remember you?"

I shrugged. "She would have overheard me now say I remember her."

"The room is soundproof," Sledge said. "Is she a threat to you?"

Lorcan stepped forward as though he wanted to put himself between me and the woman. It was an odd thing for the Fae Prince to do. I shot him a glare. He stepped back a fraction, but the tension didn't leave his body.

"No. We had no animosity toward each other. If she remembers me, it would be like I remember her, just a face I saw around town sometimes."

"I don't like this," Lorcan said. "It seems too coincidental for this woman and you to be here from the same location."

"Are you saying I'm the one who's conspiring with her?"

"Why would you jump to the assumption unless you are the one?" Lorcan asked.

I slapped his face before I even registered my hand was moving. The slap of my palm on his flesh made a loud ringing noise and my wrist hurt, but a second later the two Fae guards had me in their arms and wrenched me away from Lorcan.

"Stand down," Lorcan said.

"Release her this instant," Sledge growled the words.

The sudden surge in power coming from both men made the guards drop their hold. I rubbed my arms and stepped away from all the testosterone in the small area outside the interrogation room.

"You tell your men to never touch her again," Sledge said, the growl still clear in his voice.

One of them opened their mouth. Lorcan held up his hand to stop him from talking. His palm glowed a luminous shade of blue-green drawing my gaze like a moth to a flame. The immense power coming from him surged like it would burn the building to the ground if he set it free.

"They won't," Lorcan said.

Sledge pointed his finger. "They better not, because brother-in-law or not, no one hurts my family."

There went the warm glow in my heart again.

"I have no intention of hurting her," Lorcan said. "If anyone does, then I'll be beside you in getting retribution."

Ah, hell, my entire chest was glowing with warmth now. I'd never experienced this utmost sacred family aspect in my life. My parents had been absent most of my life working for others and selling their magical potions and spells until the day they died. The rest of my family had died in similar ways. The coven was full of selfish witches, especially the High Priestess. They'd shown no family values. And the few times I'd spent in Sledge's presence before hadn't prepared me for the length wolf shifters went to protect their family. I'd never seen it in action either. If I didn't do something else, then I'd throw myself into their arms and beg them to include me in their family just so I'd keep experiencing this warmth. This love. I shook my head and cleared my throat. Doing what I did best, I shoved my attitude to the forefront.

"Can we get this over and done with already? I want to go home."

Sledge and Lorcan exchanged a glance, then Sledge opened the door. We walked inside, leaving the guards outside since the room wasn't very large. Eloise sat handcuffed to the table in the center of the room. They'd welded the table to the floor. Even with her wolf shifter strength, she wouldn't get free.

"Sledge," Eloise said, attempting to sit up straighter and smile enticingly. "I haven't seen you for so long."

"Quit playing games, Eloise, and tell me who you're working with," Sledge said.

"I'm not working with anyone." She giggled.

"Screw this," I said. "One of you grab her head, the other open her jaw."

"Wait. Who are you?"

Sledge stepped behind Eloise and held her head. Lorcan wrenched open her jaw so hard it cracked. I didn't waste time. I popped the lid on the truth serum and dumped the contents in her mouth. Lorcan snapped her jaw shut and covered her mouth and nose with his hand. Ruthless. My impression of him went up a notch. They waited until she'd swallowed before they stepped away from her. Sledge wiped his hands on his pants as though touching her had put dirt on him. I hated he had to be in here after what happened between him and Eloise and how it upset Briana, but being the Alpha meant he had to put the pack's needs first. I understood the wolf shifter system since I had a fraction of their blood running through my veins.

"How long will it take?" Lorcan asked.

"A minute. Two tops." I settled in the chair opposite Eloise.

Lorcan paced to a corner of the room and crossed his arms. His hands glowed again. It was thrilling to see the immense power of a Fae Prince so close to me. What would his hands touch like when they were aglow? How much power did he possess? I longed to ask him those questions, but they weren't my place to ask. Neither was this the right place.

Sledge yanked out the other chair and sat beside me.

"I need to say a spell too," I said, drawing out a candle from my pouch.

The candle flickered to life as though by an invisible force. I lifted my gaze to Lorcan, but he hadn't moved. Did he light the candle from that distance? Without even moving a muscle? I wanted to experience more of his powers. The insidious ideas crept into my head. No wonder some humans wanted to harness those powers for themselves.

Closing my eyes, I chanted,

"For those that want.

The truth revealed,

And secrets unsealed,

From now until the magic ends,

Let them flow freely.

From the traitor's mouth,

To our ears

In this room

For I seek the truth."

Eloise's head snapped back. Pink tears streamed from her eyes and foam bubbled at the side of her mouth. Did I add too much belladonna to the potion? Was she about to die before we got the truth from her?

"What's happening?" Lorcan asked, stepping forward.

Eloise's head snapped forward, and she laughed. "You witches are all the same. Pretending to be powerful when you're nothing. No one wants you."

Her words were like shards in my heart. It was like she'd read my mind and poured all my insecurities over my body and lit me on fire.

"Tell us the truth, Eloise," Sledge said.

"I just did." She wiped her chin on her shoulder awkwardly while chained to the table.

"About why you attacked my father," Sledge gritted out between his clenched jaw.

"Oh, that." She laughed again.

Was she maniacal? Had I got the truth serum ingredients wrong?

"I want power," Eloise said.

Lorcan's body stiffened. His hands glowed even more.

"You said that already," Sledge said. "Tell me who told you to come here?"

"My pack Alpha. He swapped me for one of your males."

"I'm aware of the exchange," Sledge said.

I placed a hand on Sledge's arm. "You're asking them the wrong way. Let me try?"

He nodded, and I leaned forward onto the desk. Eloise bared her teeth at me. I hoped I was right, and he was asking them in the wrong way, and I hadn't got the serum wrong.

"Eloise, who helped you take down Sledge's father?"

"A man," she said, her eyes glazed over.

"What's the man's name?"

"He doesn't have a name."

"What does he look like?"

"He's short. Skinny. Flesh and bones. His eyes sink into his skull. He reminded me of those zombies you see in the movies. He stank like a rotting corpse."

I shot Sledge a look. *What the hell?*

"What did he tell you to do?"

"He told me if I wanted power, then I had to take it. He intended to take the power he'd sought to take before. I asked him what he meant, but he rambled on about fire and death."

My nightmare barreled into my mind.

"Whose fire and death?"

"He didn't say."

Was it mine he was talking about? I didn't have power though, so I didn't understand if it connected my nightmare to this. Maybe I had it all wrong and my nightmare was a dream and not a premonition.

"Ask her about Fae," Lorcan said.

"Fae," she hissed.

"Tell me what the man said about the Fae," I asked.

Her head whipped side to side as though someone was slapping her face.

"He said they're evil. They want to destroy us so he will destroy them first."

"What the fuck?" Sledge jumped to his feet. "How does this man know about the Fae? They've been missing from Earth for so long that no one should recognize them."

"I've heard rumors there were Fae left behind on Earth," I said.

"What?" Lorcan stepped closer to me. "Where?"

I shrugged.

"England," Eloise said.

"Are there Fae in England?" I asked her.

"Yes." Her eyes rolled back in her head then rolled back again.

Lorcan's hands glowed so much with his power the room was one giant-looking blue-green fireball reminding me of my dream. I sucked in a calming breath. There was no fire here. No chance of me being burned alive.

"Where are they?" I asked.

"I don't know."

"Does the man know?"

"No. He can't find where they're hidden. It's why he was here. He sensed the power of a Fae being used."

"Who the hell is he?" I leaned across the table and grabbed her top in my hands.

Why did I care so much? The Fae wasn't my concern, but the overwhelming need to protect them filled me out of nowhere. Perhaps it was the fact Sledge had mated with a Fae and by extension of him, they were now a distant relation to me. I wouldn't let myself think it was because of Lorcan and the way I wanted him.

"I don't know." More pink tears slid from her eyes.

"Where does he live?" I shook her body.

"I don't know."

"Where did you meet?"

"In the forest. At the large boulder that looks like a rat."

"The rock is near here," Sledge said. "I'll see if I can track his scent."

"Will he hurt the wolf shifters?" I asked, concerned for Sledge's safety tracking this man when we didn't understand what he was or what powers he possessed. How had he tracked the use of a Fae's power? And why hadn't he attacked Saoirse if he wanted to kill all the Fae?

"No, he doesn't care about them. He thinks their powers are pointless."

Sledge growled. I had to agree with him. Wolf shifter's powers weren't pointless. They were more powerful than me.

"Will he try to break you out of jail?"

"No, he doesn't care about me either." More foam gurgled from the corners of her mouth.

I let go of her top and sat back down. "Is there anything else you want me to ask her?"

"Is the man alone?" Lorcan asked.

"Yes," Eloise answered him. "He said he's the last of his kind and he'll get revenge."

Lorcan's face turned white. Why did he look like he was about to pass out? His hand went to his side, and he rubbed his palm back and forth.

With nothing else to ask, Sledge looked as pale as Lorcan. They stared at each other as though they were talking mind to mind but it wasn't possible. Wolf shifters didn't possess the ability of telepathy and neither did Fae. Whatever it was, neither of them appeared happy. In fact, they both appeared terrified. For these two powerful men to be scared, then it made me tremble in my chair.

Eloise slumped forward, her head banging on the desk. Foam gurgled from her mouth onto the table in a stream creating a puddle that started white and then turned red.

"Shit," I said.

"What is it?" Lorcan asked.

"I must have put too much belladonna in the serum."

Lorcan lifted her head. "She's dead."

CHAPTER TEN
LORCAN

H AD THE WITCH KILLED the traitor on purpose? Was she, as I'd suspected, the one working with Eloise? It didn't add up though. Neither did her admission she didn't have a grimoire with the correct dosage for a wolf shifter. If she was related to Sledge, then her family's grimoire would contain spells that would work on wolf shifters. There could be no room for error in a spell with one containing the ingredient belladonna.

I assessed the witch in more detail. She was guilty, or she was innocent going by the blank expression on her face.

"Why are you and Lorcan so freaked out by what she said?" Pepper asked Sledge.

Sledge's gaze met mine. He wouldn't tell her our family's secrets. The ones he would have seen when Briana placed her Fae mating mark on him. At the moment of marking, Sledge would have seen all of Briana's memories. He would jump to the same conclusion as me about who the man was.

It made no sense though. We'd killed all the Trappers. I was sure of it. The potion Saltine had given me made sure I'd find them all. I paced back and forth in the small room. My mind whirled.

"I don't believe her," I said.

"Eloise?" Pepper asked.

"Aye."

"She was under a truth serum."

"Was she?" I cocked an eyebrow.

"Are you calling me a liar again?" She pushed back her chair and stood. Her knuckles curled and uncurled as though she wanted to slap me again.

"How can we be sure you're not the one who was working with Eloise? Perhaps the serum was a ruse to throw us off your scent. That's why you killed her." I stopped pacing and faced her.

Her way too-pretty face turned red. "You're unbelievable!"

"Why, because I figured it out?"

She pointed a finger at me. "What made you so jaded? I'm not the evil one here. I attempted to help you, and this is the thanks I get." She huffed. "I'm out of here."

With a surge of my power, I slammed it into the door and sent a wall of vines to block her exit.

"I can rip them away," she said and placed her hands on the closest branch, she ripped the vines away, but I threw more power into them adding more and more leafy growth as her fingers tore relentlessly at the plants.

"All right," Sledge said, pulling Pepper away from the door. "You two are ridiculous."

He chastised us like we were little children. I suppose I was acting childish, but the witch made me experience things I shouldn't for one of her kind.

"He started it," Pepper sulked.

"Yes, and I'm finishing it." Sledge crossed his massive arms. "You both are aware I can scent lies so I'm certain Pepper had nothing to do with Eloise and what Eloise said today was true."

My fingers curled into my palms as I called my power back and dissolved the vines. I was afraid my unfounded accusation was wrong. It would have been the easiest thing all around if Pepper was the evil person. Then I could stop thinking of having her in my bed. Sprawled on my sheets, begging me to take her.

"Shite."

"Exactly," Sledge said.

"What is going on?" Pepper threw up her hands.

Sledge waited for me to speak. I paced the room again.

"What Eloise said, sounds like a Trapper," I said, not even believing I'd say such a thing.

"I thought they were dead?" Pepper frowned.

"I believed so too. I don't understand how one could still be alive after all this time?"

Pepper sat back in the chair. She eyed Eloise with a look passing for regret. Perhaps she hadn't meant to kill her after all.

"Trappers were human, right?" Pepper asked.

"Aye."

"There's no way one is alive now," Sledge said.

"Unless magic was involved," Pepper said.

Precisely what I'd been thinking. It was like she'd pulled the words from my head.

"What sort of magic?" Sledge asked.

Pepper shrugged.

"Other realms have unique magic. A human might live in certain realms and not age. They'd age the moment they left them though."

Pepper's eyebrows rose along with Sledge's.

"But a human would have to make a deal with a demon to travel to a different realm since they're the only ones who trade that service to anyone."

"Demons?" Pepper murmured.

"Mmm," I said. "They wouldn't take a human to their realm though."

"How many other realms are there?" she asked.

"A lot." I waved her question away. "But it wouldn't explain his change in appearance."

"So not another realm then?" Pepper asked.

"No. It has to be other magic." I stopped pacing and stared her in the eyes. "Witch magic."

"I hope this isn't your long-winded way of accusing me again?"

My lips twitched. As much as I didn't want to like a witch, I liked Pepper. She was never afraid to stand up to me and it made me want to push her even more to see what she'd come back with.

"No, I'm not accusing you," I said, instead.

While her slap was justified, it wasn't the sort of rebuttal I wanted from her again. No, I longed to take her in my arms and see if she was as passionate in bed as I suspected. The fact she was a witch did nothing to lessen my desire for Pepper. Nor did the protective urges and acting like an arrogant ass seem like the best defense for the sensations she was invoking in my body.

I curled my fingers into my palms. Even my powers seemed more volatile around her, but no one would see that with how well I kept them under control. Until the vines over the door that was.

"Good." She stood and fluffed the cloak. "I'll head home now."

"No," I snapped. The notion of her leaving made my heart thunder in my chest. What was this intense emotion running through me?

"No?" She scowled. "I—"

"Please stay. I will need your help to figure out what sort of magic hid a Trapper."

Her chest heaved with her deep exhale. "I wanted to sleep in my bed tonight."

"Won't you stay and help your family?" I glanced at Sledge hoping my low blow wouldn't rile him up. "Please, Pepper."

"All right. Only because you said please, but it'll cost you."

"No doubt it will. What is your price?"

She tapped a finger on her lips drawing my attention to the plump fullness I longed to kiss. The witch was torturing me, I was sure of it.

"Hmm, what can a Fae prince afford for my services?"

"Pepper," Sledge said in a warning tone.

"I suppose I can ask for a favor like I did with you, but a favor would be too easy I think." Her pretty eyes snapped toward my face and her expression softened.

She must have been thinking of something sexual because a dainty pink stole up her cheeks. I wished I could read her mind. Sledge shifted uncomfortably in his chair. Aye, the sexual tension coming from Pepper now was almost like a live current of power on my skin. I'd never had a woman make me feel this way.

"Whatever you wish," I said, my voice coming out huskier since I too was thinking of giving her whatever she desired in bed.

"Can I take a raincheck?"

I cocked my head. "What is a raincheck? You want me to make rain?"

She giggled. It was the sweetest sound I'd ever experienced in my life.

"No, silly. A raincheck is a saying which means I'll take what you owe later."

I stepped closer. "But you haven't told me what I owe."

Her tongue darted out to lick her lips. "I'll tell you when the time comes."

"You can ask for jewels." I lifted my hand and tucked a stray strand of hair back under the hood. "Emeralds, rubies, diamonds."

"Tempting," she said and swayed closer.

"Very," I agreed.

She peered up at me through her thick eyelashes. Her scent drifted around me. An earthy aroma of herbs drew me closer still.

Sledge cleared his throat. "Whatever you decide for payment, can you two do this later? I'm concerned about Saoirse and the baby."

"Me too," I said. "But I don't understand why this man hasn't attacked her if he can sense the use of Fae's power. Wouldn't he have sensed her?"

"Saoirse hasn't been alone since she's been here. There wouldn't have been the opportunity to kill her."

"I need to get her to the Summer Court today. Her and the baby. She'll be safe there."

"And I'll head to the rock and search for his scent. Pepper, come with me and see if you can sense any magic," Sledge said. "When you see Briana, make sure she stays in the Summer Court. I won't have another one of those bastards near her ever again."

"Agreed," I said. "Briana has been through enough."

"What happened to your mate?" Pepper asked Sledge.

"Long story," Sledge said. "I'll tell you later. We need to take action now before it's too late."

"Saoirse has been here months," Pepper pointed out.

"And who knows how long this man has been plotting his revenge and what he might have in store?"

CHAPTER ELEVEN
LORCAN

I DIDN'T MENTION WHAT Eloise said to Patrick and Declan. They would ask questions about my Trapper tracking ability. It was another question going through my mind. Why, if there was a Trapper on Earth, wasn't I able to sense them? I needed to travel to the Summer Court and read through Saltine's grimoire again. As many times as I'd read the book, maybe there was something I missed. Perhaps the magic had worn off. If it had, then it was even more imperative I get Saoirse and Ailbhe back in the Summer Court.

I left Sledge and Pepper to make the arrangements for their task. Each step away from Pepper seemed like my insides were being ripped away and laid before her feet. I didn't understand this sensation churning my body. Her hips swayed with each step making me stare after her and hope she meant whatever I owed her I'd have to repay in bed.

Now there was an idea I'd enjoy.

Patrick and Declan walked with me through the forest to Saoirse's cabin. Our feet crunched the eucalyptus leaves sending up a perfumed scent that didn't exist in the Summer Court except for here. On Earth, those trees flourished. A lot like the wolf shifters. This town reminded me of home. The way they all looked out for each other. It was no wonder Saoirse had made her life here with her mate.

Saoirse stood outside the cabin, her back to us as she and Arrow spared with swords. Ailbhe gurgled happily from a pram on the porch. It was good to see her keeping her skills up, but then I never considered she'd stop her sparring. She loved it too much.

Their swords clashed with a loud clang. Saoirse twirled a pirouette more like a dancer than a fighter. She was light on her feet—the reason she always won sword fights. No one ever expected her to be so fast and efficient with her strikes. She landed a pretend kill strike on Arrow. They stopped sparring when they sensed my presence.

"Don't worry, she lets no one win," I said.

Arrow smiled. "I love her competitiveness."

Saoirse stood on her tiptoes and kissed his cheek.

"If you two have finished sparring, shall we head to the Summer Court?" I asked in as cavalier a manner as possible even when my insides were churning with an urgency to get her to safety.

At least I had Patrick and Declan with me. I wordlessly thanked Father for forcing the guards to accompany me.

Their extra eyes on the surrounding forest stopped me from breaching the Veil and tossing Saoirse through.

"Now?" she asked.

"Might as well get it over with otherwise you'll become more worried."

"All right." She shoved a lock of hair away from her sweaty face. "We'll shower and change. Can you watch Ailbhe?"

"Of course."

I followed them up the stairs to the porch. They disappeared through the door, and I squatted in front of Ailbhe in the pram.

"Did you like the sword fight?"

The baby gurgled and waved his little arms.

"It sounds like you did." I chuckled. "Don't worry, your mother will teach you when you're old enough to hold a sword."

He waved his arms even more as though telling me he was strong enough now. I ran a hand over his head. Would he get a Fae crown? I touched my crown. What age had I been when the crown formed? It was when I'd been able to control my power enough, so I didn't wreak havoc on the palace. Five, maybe six years old. In Fae terms still an infant. My palm glowed with my power making Ailbhe's small head glow too. His eyes glowed next. Flittering between the indigo and blue of a Fae and the same golden hue of his father.

"What an interesting combination," I whispered to the babe. "Can you hear lies like a wolf shifter? Do you have the powers of a Fae royal too? Will you shift shape?"

Ailbhe babbled excitedly so much so he blew bubbles.

I laughed. I never contemplated I wanted children, but this little prince made me want a baby of my own. How ridiculous when I didn't have a mate. Nor did I want one.

Saoirse and Arrow walked out of the cabin looking refreshed.

"I'm coming too," Arrow said.

"I expected as much."

Saoirse unbuckled Ailbhe from the pram and hoisted him onto her hip.

"I'll open the Veil. Make sure you stay connected to Saoirse otherwise, you'll become lost in the Veil."

Saoirse grabbed his hand in a firm grip. "I'll never let go."

"Me either," Arrow said.

I nodded and drew on my power, calling to the doorway Father had created. Before us, the air shimmered in a blue-green glow. The Veil vibrated with power and the magic of the Fae. I stepped inside and waited for the others to join me. With a wave of my hand, I sealed the Veil behind us. I resisted the urge to sigh in relief. Saoirse was unaware of the potential chance there was a Trapper left. If I told her, then she might have felt I'd forced her to return to the Summer Court instead of going by her own free will and reconciling with Father.

The Veil pulsed with magical energy around us. Arrow shivered but held Saoirse tight in his arms as he kept his family together.

We stepped out of the Veil into the tower of the Summer Court. The guards rushed forward as though we were a threat, but their demeanor changed the second they comprehended who we were. I wasn't sure how we were going to explain Saoirse's baby considering the Veil was supposed to be locked until a short time ago, but that was Father's problem. The guards whispered amongst themselves. Looks like the proverbial wolf was out of the bag.

There hadn't been a wolf shifter in the Summer Court for hundreds of years. No one appeared to want to talk to us. I told Patrick and Declan to head back to the barracks and catch up on their sleep. I doubted they'd had much while on Earth. They took their jobs way too seriously to have rested properly, and I'd be heading back as soon as possible. No doubt Father would insist I take them with me again.

I still hadn't resolved if I'd tell everyone about Eloise and what she said.

Saoirse and Arrow were quiet as we walked toward the palace. Arrow's eyes were enormous as he peered at the Summer Court for the first time in real life. He would have seen the place when he witnessed Saoirse's memories but experiencing it in person was different. The Summer Court always had a happiness to it that seeped into your soul. It brought you peace and comfort.

The sky was a glorious blue as usual. Faint clouds drifted across the horizon. The fields rustled in the breeze. I inhaled a calming breath of the place that was my home. For the first time in my many years, it didn't feel like I'd come home. I tried not to frown. What was wrong with me?

The palace appeared ahead. Tall and majestic as it always was. It glistened in the sunshine as though made from a billion gems. The doors to the palace opened and Grier nodded at us. His expression gave nothing away as he gawked at Saoirse, the baby, then Arrow. Perhaps Father had told him what had transpired?

"His Majesty is in the library with your mother."

"We'll head there," I said. "No need to announce us."

Mother would be so happy when she saw Saoirse and her grandson. Ailbhe squirmed in Saoirse's arms. Arrow extracted him from her tight hold. I placed my hand in Saoirse's and squeezed it.

"Stay," she whispered.

"I'll be by your side," I said.

She nodded but held my hand in a firm grip.

I opened the library doors with my free hand. Mother was the first to see us. She launched herself at us in a run so fast she was a blur of flying purple fabric. One second Saoirse's hand was in mine, the next it was around Mother's back holding her close while they both cried. Father's gaze met mine, and he nodded his thanks. He stood back and let Mother and Saoirse reconnect.

Ailbhe let out a squawk. Arrow bounced him up and down, but the baby was determined to be the center of attention.

"My," Mother said, placing a hand on her chest. "He looks like you did as a baby, Saoirse. May I hold him?"

"I think he might scream the place down if you don't," Arrow said and placed the baby in Mother's arms.

She beamed in happiness and touched a reverent finger to his lips. The baby quietened and placed a finger on Mother's lips. Mother's grin grew even more.

"He's beautiful," Mother said, with a wistful sigh. "Thank you for coming and bringing him." She turned to Arrow. "You must be my daughter's mate."

"I am," Arrow said. "I'm Arrow Goldstein. It's a pleasure to meet you, Your Majesty."

"None of that now. Call me Niamh when we're inside the palace."

"Saoirse?" Father asked.

I'd never seen the Fae King so unsure of anything in his life. He had reason to be though. Saoirse turned.

Father fell to his knees, tears streaming down his face. "Forgive me?"

Saoirse launched herself into him. He wrapped her up in his arms almost swallowing her entire body with the way he held her. They rocked side to side. Mother hummed a soothing tune letting a small amount of her unusual Fae power fill the room. Saoirse wiped the back of her hands over her eyes. Father scrubbed his face dry.

"I'm so sorry," Father whispered. "I was wrong."

CHAPTER TWELVE
PEPPER

"WHAT'S UP WITH YOU and Lorcan?" Sledge asked as we made our way through the forest.

Trees loomed overhead, but the forest wasn't as thick this far away from Crystal Creek. The undergrowth was sparser and easier to traverse. Reddish-brown rocks littered the landscape in small boulders the size of a baseball. They were rounded and perfect as though a river had once flowed through the area many, many years ago. Were we in what once was a riverbed? It would explain the gently undulating path we seemed to follow.

"Nothing."

I pushed a branch aside and let it fling back in Sledge's face except his reflexes were too fast and he caught the branch before it wiped the smug smile from his face.

"Nothing my ass," Sledge said. "You two act like you hate each other but you secretly want to tear each other's clothes off."

I spun with a start. "How did you pick up on that?"

He laughed.

"Shit."

I stomped off but I couldn't match the speed of a wolf shifter. He placed a restraining hand on my shoulder.

"Wait."

"What is it?"

"The rock is up ahead. I want to get a good whiff before you step closer."

"Hey, I don't stink."

"You do." He laughed. "But everyone does to a wolf shifter."

I folded my arms. "Why don't I have your sense of smell? I'm part wolf shifter."

"Not enough I guess." He shrugged. "I'm going to shift so I can search better."

"Fine." I settled on the ground facing the other direction. "I'll wait here. Call out if you need help."

I placed a hand inside my pouch and touched all the potions I'd brought with me. There was a smoke screen which, when thrown on the ground, would explode and release a vast cloud of thick smoke. For a moment, it would confuse someone. A round vial held a stun potion when I said a spell too. It would incapacitate a person for a good hour. It was one I didn't get to use often, so I hoped I'd get the chance today. There were a few others, too.

The rustle of clothes being removed was loud in the quiet forest. Come to think of it, there wasn't any bird or animal noises in this area.

"Sledge, did you notice the lack of noise?"

A damp nose poked my cheek. Sledge's big black wolf looked down into my eyes. His head bobbed as though he agreed with me.

"Be careful."

His dark lids blinked over his brilliant blue eyes even in wolf form then he stalked into the forest. I scooted around on my bottom and surveyed his black form disappear amongst the many trees and bushes. Why was I so concerned about his welfare? He was an Alpha wolf shifter. He'd look after himself. I was nothing but a witch with basic magic skills.

Sledge's footfalls were nonexistent. Was it his skill in his stalking or was magic surrounding this place? Magic, I didn't sense from here. Time ticked away and my nerves fluttered in anxiety. I rose to my feet ready to find out if Sledge was okay. His dark shadow flitted through the bushes, and he bounded up to me with his tail wagging.

A sigh of relief left my lungs. The black wolf yipped at me. I turned around for Sledge to shift and redress. I didn't need to see my relative naked, and it appeared he felt the same way even though a shifter would be used to nudity.

"There was no scent," Sledge said. "The closer I got to the rock all the scents of the forest vanished."

"A magical protection spell then."

"Or barrier like the one at our waterfall."

"What is going on in your town? Why are there so many magical barriers?"

"I have no freaking clue, but I want to find out."

"Me too. Show me to the rock."

Sledge led the way through the forest until we came upon a reddish-brown rock the size of a truck. It had a large, pointed end resembling a rat's nose. The rock rose in a gradual incline then rounded out and dipped back down. It didn't end there though. The rock formed a long line close to the ground which was like a rat's tail.

"I suppose it looks like a rat, but who came up with that in the first place?"

"Local kids was the story I was told," Sledge said.

I lifted my palms and stepped closer to the rocks. Magic vibrated. Strong. Impenetrable. I cocked my head. Or that's what the one who'd placed it there believed. This wasn't like the barrier the Fae King forced between our two worlds. This was different.

"Well?" Sledge asked.

"It's a barrier. An old one. No one has kept the magic up to date so with the right spells and potions I might breech it."

"What will you need?"

"I'll have to consult my grimoire, but I might get it wrong like the way I did the potion for Eloise."

"What's the worst that could happen?" Sledge asked.

"Instead of opening it, I'd blow it up. And us with it."

CHAPTER THIRTEEN
LORCAN

I SAT IN THE library with my family. A familiar place inside the palace. Wall-to-wall shelves of books stretched to the ceiling and a ladder reached the higher shelves. It wasn't as impressive as the library in the village, but there were still many books to read. My thoughts kept wandering back to Pepper though. To the way she intrigued me. The way I hungered to kiss her more than I had any woman before her. But I stayed for as long as it took for Saoirse to be comfortable back here. It'd taken longer than I'd assumed. Even after Father's apology, Saoirse appeared reserved. Arrow had helped mend the break in our family, which was a surprise since he was so protective of his mate. I sensed he'd rather put an end to anyone who had hurt her rather than play peacekeeper.

Ailbhe was the one who brought the change the most.

The moment the Fae King held him in his arms, Ailbhe's little hands glowed in a rainbow hue of power.

The connection to our ancestors hummed in his body so much that I considered Father would cry again.

"This day calls for a celebration," I said, for I couldn't sit here indefinitely. "We should have a family party. I'll fetch Rian and Sophia."

"Agreed," Mother said, standing. "I'll ask the cooks to make us a feast."

She disappeared from the room so fast, Father didn't have time to say no. Not that he would. He always gave in to his mate.

Father frowned. "I can send a guard to fetch Rian and Sophia."

"I'd like to visit him and see where he's living now."

My excuse was part of the reason. I also wanted to talk to Rian alone without the prying ears of my family. Talk to him about a witch who wouldn't leave my thoughts.

"Take the guards with you," he said, still holding Ailbhe on his lap like he didn't believe the miracle before him.

"Aye."

I had expected nothing less from him, it's why I'd sent Patrick and Declan to rest. They wouldn't be happy about going back to Earth so soon. Nor would they be happy when we went back to Crystal Creek alone. I still hadn't figured out what to say to keep Saoirse here besides the truth and if I told them all there might be the possibility of a Trapper being alive, then Father might lose his mind again, and Saoirse might think I'd tricked her back to the Summer Court. I stood to leave.

"Hurry back," Saoirse said, staring at me as though I'd broken my promise.

Mother returned to the room and Saoirse smiled. I guess she didn't want to be left alone with Father yet.

"Your sisters are on their way," Mother said.

"I can't wait to see them all," Saoirse said.

Time for me to leave before they all swarmed Saoirse and Ailbhe, as well as meeting Arrow. Saoirse would be fine without me. Briana would be here soon, and she was almost as protective of Saoirse as I was. She'd been by Saoirse's side when she'd given birth. Going against Father's wishes had become a family trait in recent times.

I left the palace and made my way to the army barracks. The guards greeted me in their usual way, but the second I walked by them, they whispered behind my back. Of course, Saoirse turning up in the Summer Court with a wolf shifter mate and a baby would cause them to talk. I wasn't about to add to their rumors by confirming or denying she'd left the Summer Court before the Fae King created the doorway.

Patrick and Declan were none too pleased we were heading back to Earth, but they strapped on their swords and donned their boots. We made our way to the field and the tower holding the doorway.

"Back already?" Cashel, the guard on duty asked.

"Aye, we're heading to Rian in the Amazon."

"Very well," Cashel nodded at the scribe who jotted down our destination.

It stung to have my whereabouts kept a record so closely. Until a short time ago, I'd flitted back and forth through the Veil with no one aware of where I was. Foolish now there was the threat of a Trapper still being alive. I'd been so certain they were all dead. Even when my brother and sisters said they wanted to breach the locked Veil in secret, I'd made sure I'd checked Earth first before they went through.

I stepped into the Veil once again, letting the power behind the magic surround my body in a sparkling mist. Patrick and Declan joined me. I searched through many locations until I found the thread to take me to Rian. We stepped into the Amazon jungle. Green for as far as we could see. Thick fernery surrounded us. The fronds of the leaves tickled against our hands. Overhead, tall trees stretched so high in the air that my neck ached to look at the heights they grew to. The trees in the Summer Court were taller, but they were golden with silver bark. Here the bark was darker and with the shadows of the foliage hiding the sun from sight, everything appeared darker still. The earthy scents of rain and leaves surrounded us in a combination that wasn't unwelcome.

Birds squawked and launched themselves into the sky in a flurry of brightly colored feathers leaving the thick jungle behind. A jaguar roared from behind us. The sound echoed through the forest. Patrick and Declan drew their swords.

"Stand down. You're aware Rian mated with a jaguar shifter."

Another rumbling roar filled the jungle. All other noises ceased as the animals considered the predator stalking its prey. Except we weren't prey. We were now family.

"I'm Lorcan, Rian's brother," I called out.

The black jaguar stalked through the thick undergrowth and paced in front of us. Its tail twitched from side to side as it assessed me and the guards. The enormous cat stalked away, then paused, turning its head to see if we were following. We fell into step behind the jaguar. Patrick placed himself between me and the cat while Declan placed himself behind me.

The steamy air in the jungle made sweat drip down my skin. I wiped my forehead and inhaled the thick air. This place was so different from the Summer Court. At least Crystal Creek hadn't been this humid. Here it seemed as though I was walking through a wall of moisture with each step. The palm fronds parted, and a village of treehouses came into view. People were everywhere. Some were building more treehouses, and others were cooking on an open firepit. Fae guards dressed in green instead of red stood guard alongside jaguar shifters. They halted us on the outskirts of the village.

"State your business," the jaguar shifter said.

"I'm Lorcan, Fae Prince of the Summer Court. I'm here to speak with my brother Rian and his mate Sophia."

The Fae guard grinned. "Lorcan, Patrick, Declan, so good to see you."

"You too, Flynn."

"I'll take you to King Rian."

"King?" I raised my eyebrows.

"He's the mate to the Queen of the Jungle so he's king here," Flynn said leading us toward a treehouse. "Mind you, the jaguar shifters put their queen first, but they've accepted us with open arms. It's almost like old times being back here on Earth. Here we are." He stopped at the bottom of the largest tree in the village.

A rope ladder hung from the platform above. Flynn climbed the ladder.

"Wait here," I said to Patrick and Declan.

They didn't look happy but as good guards, they did what I said. I climbed the rope ladder and stood on the platform. The view from the top of the gigantic tree spanned across the treetops and the village. Flynn knocked on the door and a moment later, Rian opened it.

"Lorcan!"

"Hello, brother."

His brows tugged into a frown. "Come in."

I nodded at Flynn, who descended the rope ladder, then I stepped into Rian's new home. The treehouse was basic, but it had a homely atmosphere to it with plants flowering inside to soothe any Fae. Rian pointed at the timber table and chairs, so we sat.

"What's wrong?"

"Nothing."

He placed his elbows on the table and rested his chin in his hands. "I can see it in your eyes."

I glanced away. "Where's Sophia?"

"She's outside. We have privacy up here. If you're worried about anyone overhearing, they won't."

"I am. Everything is a mess."

"How so?" he asked.

"What's it like here?" I asked instead of answering him.

"Good. There are difficulties, but we expected the reintegration back to Earth to come with a learning curve. Now stop changing the subject and tell me what's going on."

"Father tasked me to bring Saoirse home."

"Aye. She didn't go?"

"No. She's at the Summer Court now. I came to fetch you too so we can have a family celebration."

"Of course, we'll go," he said. "Did Ciara find anything for you to search the waterfall while you were there?"

"No." I frowned.

"Is that what's troubling you?"

Should I tell Rian there might be a Trapper alive and after revenge? He appeared at ease here. Happy too. I didn't want to ruin the happiness he'd found with his mate. He didn't need to be aware of the threat. I'd take care of the Trapper myself.

"I met a witch."

"So?"

"I... she's infuriating. I don't like her, but I want her."

Rian chuckled.

"It's not funny. How can I want a witch after everything they did to the Fae?"

"They weren't the ones who killed us."

"No, but they gave the Trappers the means they needed to incapacitate us. How do I get over their part in the deaths?"

Rian sighed. "It's hard to forgive the past, but this witch wouldn't have been alive back then. She wouldn't have been the one to sell her potions to trap us. She's not at fault here."

"Maybe not, but her family might have played a part."

"Perhaps, but you'd never know for certain, and would you hold her accountable for the sins of her ancestors if they had?"

"I have been thinking it was her fault. I can't stand knowing witch's potions were instrumental in our massacre."

"If you can't get over the past, then you have no right to want her in your life. Let her be."

"And if I can't?"

"Then you have to forgive."

I rubbed my forehead. "I can't stop thinking about her. It's an obsession."

Rian's lips spread into a smirk.

"What?"

He chuckled. "You and Saoirse are so like each other."

"Why would you say that now?"

"She didn't realize she'd met her fated mate."

I shoved back my chair so fast it tumbled over onto the floor with a thud.

"No way. A witch can't be my fated mate."

"The same way a wolf shifter couldn't be Saoirse's or Briana's fated mate, or the way a jaguar shifter couldn't be mine?" He cocked an eyebrow.

"No, because those can take a Fae mating mark. A witch wouldn't live through it. So, this obsession I have with Pepper is nothing but lust."

"Whatever you say, Lorcan."

"Think about it," I said. "If I marked her, she'd never wake at best, die at worst. What sort of fated mate would it make me if I put her in a coma or killed her?"

"Fate sends us our mate." He dropped his hands on the table. "The trouble with you is, you don't want one whereas I did. It's why I recognized Sophia was mine the second I met her. It wouldn't have mattered what she was, I would have made it work."

I narrowed my eyes. "Who says I don't want a mate?"

"The long line of Fae women in the Summer Court can attest to my assumption."

I snapped my lips shut. He had a point, and he'd told the truth. I didn't want a mate. I didn't want anyone to know my darkest memories. No one but me deserved to suffer those. Rian didn't understand. He'd stayed in the Summer Court while I'd doled out death to the Trappers.

He stood and slapped me on the shoulder. "Let's hope your future fated mate won't hold your long line of women against you."

"Shut up." I scowled. "I don't have a fated mate."

Rian laughed harder.

I scowled deeper. Was I against having a fated mate? If I met her, surely I'd know who my fated mate was. What if Rian was right? And I was too scared to realize? Was Pepper my fated mate?

CHAPTER FOURTEEN

LORCAN

S OPHIA DIDN'T EVEN QUESTION Rian when he said they needed to head to the Summer Court. Her devotion made me think having a fated mate wouldn't be terrible. She'd given out orders like a true queen of her people and clasped Rian's hand in hers as he walked her through the Veil. As we returned once again to the Summer Court, we made our progression to the palace.

Grier flung open the door and grinned wide.

"Everyone is in the ballroom," he said.

Rian and I exchanged a smile. Trust Mother and Father to make the celebration even grander than a feast. We walked along the grand marble hallways to the ballroom. Sophia and Rian chatted happily as though they hadn't just left the depths of the Amazon jungle and arrived in an opulent palace. The pair seemed to take everything in their stride. Was that another thing fated mates did for each other? If Pepper was truly mine as Rian suspected, then would she walk the hallways of the palace by my side? How would that be possible when there was so much history between our species? I rubbed my hip where the mark resided as I contemplated the impossible. We passed the opening to the atrium housing our Spring Baile. The magic inside called a seductive song to me.

"I'll join you in a minute," I said, ducking into the atrium.

Rian and Sophia kept walking. He must have sensed I needed a moment alone to gather my thoughts. I crossed the cobblestones to the boulders lining the subtly rippling water. The scent of the fresh water drifted up and mingled with the blooms hanging from the ceiling. I stared at the water wishing it was as it used to be, but the still flowing spring helped settle the swirling of my power. The way the spring's current had decreased in recent times was a cause for concern. Our immortality was connected to the water. If the spring ceased to flow, we'd become mortal, wither, and die as humans did on Earth. No Fae wanted to die.

Around my head hung the perfumed blooms drooping from the ceiling. They became more fragrant as though they'd released fresh flowers. Through a gap in the ceiling, the sun shone onto the water making it sparkle as though a million fireflies lived beneath the surface. It wasn't true, as the array of colored pebbles through the crystal-clear water could attest to that magical illusion. Still, the place was the most beautiful in the kingdom. Any realm in my opinion. What would Pepper think of our spring?

Father walked through the opening and joined me in the atrium. "What bothers you?"

"Too much."

He kneeled on a large boulder and placed his hand in the water. The glow intensified as he fed his power into the spring. Suddenly, the water gurgled with more speed.

"You're feeding the spring your power?"

"I am. It only gives it a momentary burst of renewed vigor though."

Father's shoulders slumped. "You children believe there is a cure on Earth. Are you close to finding it?"

"I believe Ciara has been studying hard and is close to a breakthrough."

"Ah, she is smart."

"Book smart," I said, for she was.

Ciara spent most of her time in the library in the village studying every book many times over. From what Rian said, he'd given her new information which might lead her to a discovery.

"Aye," Father said. "While you are smart in your way."

I sighed. "I don't feel smart some days, Father."

"We all have days like those. Remember those days for they humble us on the days we believe we are invincible."

I grimaced. "You and I both understand we're not invincible."

"No, but we are hard to kill."

"Not hard enough," I muttered.

"Are we in danger?" His hands sparked with enough power that the entire atrium lit up as if the sun had fallen through the opening.

"If I said I needed to go back to Earth alone, would you allow me?"

His head twitched to the side.

"I would say no, but then, that never stopped you from going there alone before, did it?"

A small smile crept onto my lips. Out of all of his offspring, I understood Father the most. Perhaps I was the most like him. Or maybe it was the night we'd exacted revenge that brought us closer. "No, it didn't."

"Why would you need to go alone?"

Pepper. She was the immediate reason that popped into my head. Her beautiful face. Her red lips. The sass that came out of her mouth. The way her body swayed under her cloak. Everything about her made me want to learn more.

"Ah, you met a woman." He dipped his head. "I think a week-long celebration is in order, don't you?" he asked with a mischievous twinkle in his eyes.

If guests overran the palace partying all day and night, then no one would notice my absence as much. Father had handed me what I needed to see Pepper again. And what should be more important, to check if there was a Trapper still alive.

"Aye," I said. "I think a week is perfect."

CHAPTER FIFTEEN
PEPPER

I KICKED MY HEELS up on the couch at Sledge's hotel and flicked through the grimoire. Try as I might, I didn't find the answer I needed to break the magical barrier around the rat rock. Sighing, I tossed the book onto the oversized couch beside me.

The front door opened, and a gust of wind blew inside making me shiver, but then I caught sight of Lorcan, and a different shiver took up residence in my body. Every nerve ending fired to life as though he'd lit an internal flame of desire.

"You're back," I said pathetically.

"Aye." He grinned.

Why did he have to look so good? So cocky too as though he understood I liked the look of him.

"Did you find anything at the rock?" he asked.

"A magical barrier. I can't figure out who made it though." I pointed at my grimoire. "This hasn't helped either."

He picked up my grimoire and sat on the couch beside me. His long fingers flicked through the pages. He moved a fraction causing his thigh to brush against mine. Sparks of arousal lit my entire body. How ridiculous one small touch turned me on.

I cleared my throat.

His gaze lifted to my face. Awareness flitted in the indigo rim so radiantly it lit the blue of his eyes into a brilliant sapphire color. Hypnotized by the change in his eyes, I leaned closer. Drawn to Lorcan like a moth willing to die for the flicker of the flame. His tongue darted along his lips. My breathing hitched. Was he about to kiss me? Put me out of the misery of wondering what his kiss was like.

His gaze dropped to my lips then rose back up to my eyes. His lips stretched into a smirk. Damn, I forgot how arrogant he was. I shifted my leg away from his by crossing it over my knee and breaking all contact with him. It lessened the racing in my heart but not the lust rolling through my body or the incessant throb between my legs.

"This grimoire isn't yours," he said, refocusing on the pages.

"No. I don't know what happened to our family grimoire."

"Whose is this?"

"The High Priestess at my old coven."

"She gave it to you?"

"No. I stole it."

"I shouldn't have expected anything less," he said with a frown.

"Look, whatever your problem is with me, you can take it and you out the door."

That way I wouldn't have to battle the urge to rub myself against him. People had treated witches poorly for such a long time, but I wouldn't sit around and let them do it to me too.

Lorcan glared at the door as though he was about to leave, then he let out a sigh and tossed the book aside. He rose and left without a word. Well, what did I expect? I'd told the Fae Prince to leave, so why did my throat close and my eyes well? Why did my heart ache with every beat as though I was in pain?

I lifted a throw pillow to my face and screamed into the thick cushion. And again. Feeling a fraction better after the release, I hugged the cushion to my chest and stared at the ceiling for a long time. It was better this way. With the Fae Prince out of sight, then I could hopefully shove him out of my mind. And get over this ridiculous crush. Obsession. Whatever it was.

The door flung open again on another flurry of wind. Dropping the cushion, I stared at Lorcan in shock.

"I thought you left."

And how had I acted?

"I did," he said. "I needed to get this from the Summer Court."

He lifted a bulky grimoire. The leather binding was ancient in his hands. He sat next to me again, and I caught sight of the family insignia on the front. Shock barreled through my body. I snatched it from his lap and traced the outline of the willow tree etched into the leather with a shaky finger.

"Where did you get this?"

"An old witch gave it to me."

"No." I stood and hugged the book to my chest. "A witch wouldn't give away their family grimoire to a stranger."

"She did, otherwise how would I have it?"

"You must have stolen it."

"Must I now?" Lorcan folded his arms over his chest. "Just because you're a thief doesn't make me one."

I glared. "She would have given it to a family member. They'd have passed the grimoire down through the generations." I sniffed. "Given it to me, not some arrogant Fae Prince who knows nothing about being a witch."

"This is your family?" He uncrossed his arms and stood.

"Yes. This is mine. All these years and you'd stolen it."

"I never stole it. Saltine Woodswillow gave it to me."

"Saltine." I gasped. "You were friends with her?"

How old was he if he'd met my great-great by many times grandmother?

"Aye. She was our witch seer."

Every drop of blood in my body drained from me. I swayed on my feet. Lorcan gathered me in his arms and lowered me to the couch. Everything in me went numb. It was true. Seer blood ran through my veins. My nightmares were premonitions. Which would mean I'd die in a blazing inferno.

"What's wrong?" Lorcan asked, placing his palm on my forehead. "Are you ill?"

I slapped his hand away. How would I trust him to tell him?

"Why did she give you the grimoire?"

"I'd rather not talk about it." He grimaced as though he'd eaten a lemon.

Grabbing his shirt in a fist, I said, "Why did you have my family legacy?"

"You're so infuriating." He huffed. "She gave it to me the night of the Trapper massacre. Father and I along with our guards sought her help. We'd learned the Trappers were using witch's magic to capture us." He paused for a moment then continued. "The Trappers had sought to get her to work for them and when she'd rejected them, they attacked her. Left her in the ruins of her cottage to die."

"No," I whispered.

"She'd seen us coming in her visions though and had potions ready for us. She gave us the protection we needed, and she gave me a potion to let me track every Trapper." He placed a hand on his hip. "How can one still be alive? I don't sense a Trapper on Earth."

My fingers tightened on his shirt. "She couldn't have died."

"Saltine told me to take care of the grimoire. She was barely alive when we left. We all thought she'd died."

"What was she like?" I asked.

He was silent a minute then he said, "She was powerful. Smart. Determined. A lot like you."

I'd heard stories of Saltine, every witch had, but more so in our family. She was a legend. A witch who was unparalleled in power. For Lorcan to say she was like me was the highest compliment he ever gave me. He wasn't so bad. Maybe I'd read him all wrong? Underneath the hostility and distrust, Lorcan had to have a heart if he'd kept my family's grimoire all these years. An heirloom he'd brought back to me.

I hauled him closer with my tight grip on his shirt and gave into the temptation to kiss him. Our lips met in a crash so great I felt it in my soul. One touch of his lips to mine and I'd lit a passion neither of us could control.

CHAPTER SIXTEEN
PEPPER

LORCAN KISSED ME LIKE a man possessed with uncontrollable desire. His wild passion inflamed mine even higher. I leaned closer. His hand slid into the back of my hair, and he drew me closer still. I fell into his body, tumbling us backward on the couch. His lips never left mine, as though magic held them together. The magic of desire. Red hot passion. I'd kissed other men, but none compared to the way the Fae Prince kissed me.

There were kisses and then there were kisses that branded your soul. His lips claimed mine, and it felt so right. Like being in Lorcan's arms was where I'd always meant to be.

My blood pounded in my veins and echoed in my ears. Lorcan's hand stayed glued to the back of my head as though he was afraid I'd break the kiss. I wouldn't. I couldn't. Each moment his lips were on mine and his tongue tangled with mine was like I'd found heaven. Or the other piece of my soul that I didn't know was missing. His other hand ran the length of my back up and down in a rhythm that was driving me to desperation. Each pass never went where I needed it. Between my legs. I longed for him to claim all of me. Every inch. Body, soul, heart.

I straddled the enormous bulge inside his pants, needing to get even closer to Lorcan. Sparks of ecstasy tingled where we touched. I rocked my hips and ground my aching flesh on his body.

We moaned at the same time. In sync with every kiss, touch, and whimper.

Lorcan's hips rolled up into mine as we continued the delicious friction I never wanted to end. His hand dipped lower over the curves of my backside. I moaned louder. So did he. His hand dipped under my t-shirt touching sparks of power and magic to my skin. He stroked the bare skin on my back sending a shiver of desire from my toes to the top of my head. Each place his hand touched ignited with a fiery passion setting my skin alight with a delicious tingle of arousal. His other hand left my head and joined the contact under my t-shirt. I lifted my chest wanting to rid myself of the restrictive material. I needed more of his touch. Hungered for it like I had with no one else.

Instead of taking off my t-shirt, he slid his hands inward and stroked the sensitive skin on my outer breasts. My nipples pebbled and ached with the need to be touched. Each touch was a torment and ecstasy. After he'd driven me to the point of almost begging, he sat up, pushed me back, and broke our kiss.

"I shouldn't do this," he whispered.

His eyes glittered so radiantly with lust, my need intensified to the heat of the blazing sun. He reached forward and stroked the exposed section of my stomach as though he could not stop himself from touching me.

"But you will," I said, because there was no doubt in my mind, I wanted him.

"Unless you tell me no." His finger stroked my stomach until every muscle clenched in need for Lorcan to dip between my legs.

"You'll only hear yes from me."

I'd barely finished my sentence, and he lifted the t-shirt over my head. His eyes heated even more as he took in my naked breasts. Lorcan stared at them as though they were the most magnificent breasts he'd ever seen. He leaned forward and pressed tender kisses against my chest as though he was worshipping the fact he uncovered them.

"More," I demanded in a husky voice.

He caught the peak of one nipple in the warmth of his mouth making my back bow in delight. His tongue flicked the hard tip yanking a cry of delight from me. He switched to the other nipple and gave it the same core-clenching treatment. His lips and tongue drove me crazy. I'd never been so turned on in my life. No human compared to the way a Fae kissed and touched me. My panties were damp between my legs, I was that aroused. I longed for Lorcan to tear my clothes from my body and bury his cock inside me. Show me with every inch of him how much more pleasure we could make together.

He placed his warm palms on my shoulders and pushed me backward on the couch. My head landed on the soft cushion as I floated on a cloud of bliss. His mouth kissed my stomach, and I sucked in an aroused breath of anticipation. Lower his lips traveled until he reached the top of my pants. His fingers dipped into the waistband and stroked the sensitive skin beneath.

"Take them off," I rasped out as my hips moved trying to get him to move lower where I needed him most.

"Shh," he said. "I'll take care of you."

My heart exploded in a pounding rhythm threatening to make me pass out. The room faded into the background as Lorcan became my center. My universe. Lorcan worshipped my body, that was the only word for it. He tugged my pants and panties down bit by bit, following each inch of revealed skin with his mouth. A kiss to each hip made my back arch. A kiss on each inner thigh made them shake in anticipation. Lower he went, kissing my knees and making me laugh because they were ticklish. He paused his descent to watch my laughter as though he enjoyed seeing it as much as hearing it. As though he cherished every moment we were together.

If I didn't know any better, I'd say he was making love to me, but he scarcely tolerated me, so this was sex. This was us giving into our basic desires. The way my heart pounded inside my chest, the way my body sang with pleasure under his hands, and the way my lips still tingled from the pressure of his, made this moment magical. As though his magic sought mine.

Lorcan smirked with his 'I'm sexy and I know it' smile, then he lowered his head and kissed my ankles. He tugged my pants free and threw them across the room sending my panties landing in one spot and my pants in another. Lorcan lifted my foot and placed a delicate kiss on my instep. Even that sent a flutter of wanting more through my body.

"I hope you don't have a foot fetish," I said.

"I have a 'you' fetish." He lowered my foot spreading my leg wide until my foot landed on the floor as he did so.

His glittering gaze landed between my legs and that, too, felt like he was claiming me. Making me his just by branding me with his eyes. He lifted my other foot and kissed the instep then lowered it, spreading me wider still so my foot rested on the top of the couch. Now he would see all of me. Every inch of my aroused flesh.

"So pink and perfect," he said.

I dropped my head back and stared at the ceiling. Watching him stare at me so intimately overwhelmed me with embarrassment he'd see how aroused he'd made me.

"Pepper," he said.

"Mmm," I mumbled.

"Watch me as I touch you for the first time."

Even his words were hotter than anything I'd ever experienced. In the deepness of his voice, the thread of command caused me to tilt my head forward and do as he said.

"Good girl."

I shivered under his praise. He ran his hands up the insides of my legs, inching closer and closer to where he'd promised to touch me. I longed for it to happen. For him to touch me in the place he gazed at with such thrall. I wanted this moment to last forever. His expression made every fiber of my being respond as though I was his alone. The tips of his fingers brushed my inner thighs. My breath stuttered in my lungs. And then they touched my sensitive flesh and spread me wide. His gaze heated even more. Became more primal. More lust ridden if that was possible.

"Mine," he said.

I nodded my head. His. Yes. I'd agree with anything he said with the way my body throbbed beneath his. The way my heart pounded in my ears with him near. The way every pulse point in my body pounded beneath his fingers as though alive with magic. He stared for a long time, but he only made me even more aroused until I felt more of my arousal coating my flesh.

Lorcan moved his thumbs first, gathering my arousal and stroking the sides of my exposed throbbing clit. My thighs trembled in time with each soft caress. He was mind-numbingly soft with his touch making each slight brush of his thumbs feel like a thousand jolts of magical power in my body.

My core clenched and unclenched as though not happy at being empty. As though begging him to bury his cock inside and make me his in every way. He must have seen it because he smirked, and it was the sexiest expression on his face. His thumbs dipped to my entrance, and I almost shot off the end of the couch with how sensitive my flesh was to his touch.

He stopped touching me and yanked my hips back toward him. "Stay still."

I bit my lip and nodded. The command in his voice was powerful. Weaved with magic that I responded to. With Lorcan touching my body, I trusted he'd take care of me which was a strange sensation to have with him of all people, after the way we'd been toward each other since meeting. The hostility was long gone now. In its place was an emotion I couldn't put a name to.

Lorcan pressed two fingers into my soaked entrance, making me forget everything that ever existed except for this moment here with him. My inner muscles clamped around his fingers as though they wanted to hold him close and never let him go. Deep inside, the tips of his fingers circled my G-spot until the desire to slam my legs shut around his hand swamped me.

"Keep them open," he said, placing his other hand under my bottom and tilting my hips upward.

"Oh, God," I cried as the new angle made his fingers brush my front wall where the hidden gems of my engorged clitoris throbbed and swelled under direct contact.

Lorcan chuckled. "I like you like this, an obedient quivering mess. Should I keep you like this for all time?"

"Yes," I said. If he made me experience this much pleasure all the time, then I'd die happy.

"Dia, Pepper, I never considered it'd be like this."

"What?" I stuttered.

He leaned forward and swiped his tongue over the engorged tip of my clit. Instead of words, a scream of ecstasy left my mouth. His tongue circled the bud until stars glittered in my eyes. His fingers moved languidly until I could no longer breathe normally. Each touch brought me closer and closer to an orgasm. To where my soul would shatter into pieces. My legs shook so hard I was afraid I'd never walk again. Deep inside the first tremors of an orgasm started, but I didn't want this ecstasy to end. I struggled to stop myself from coming, but he'd wound me too tight for too long. Lorcan's mouth and fingers lured the orgasm from my body with the promise of eternal bliss.

I came with a scream of pleasure. Of a desire to always feel this way. Cherished. Taken care of. My back bowed off the couch as every muscle inside me clamped around his fingers. Pulsing so hard my head thrashed from side to side. He stroked me through the orgasm sending another wave of pleasure through me. My legs jerked in time with my clenching muscles. Lorcan swiped his tongue over my too-sensitive clit then lifted his head to watch my face. Even more intimate than looking between my legs. He examined every line on my face as the multiple orgasms rode my body in waves of pleasure. As though he was committing the occasion to memory. Holding it close to his heart.

Lorcan kept his fingers inside me until the very last tremor left my body. My ears still rang from the intensity of the orgasms. Even my vision was a little hazy.

But an expression of regret flitted over Lorcan's face. My face flamed with shame. Had I been too wanton? Too into this and he wasn't?

I struggled to move but his hands landed on my hips.

"Oh, crap, I'm sorry, I was... I shouldn't..." A sob caught in my throat.

How had it been so special and now...

"Shh." He placed his finger over my lips.

The same finger he'd had inside me and all I smelled was my arousal and now he regretted it.

"Sledge is waiting outside."

"Oh," I said as another wave of embarrassment washed over me. "Did he see anything?"

"No, but he overheard and now he wants to rip off my head."

"I heard that," Sledge called out through the front door.

"Damn wolf shifters and their hearing," Lorcan said. "I suppose I should be grateful he waited until one of us finished."

I slithered out from under Lorcan and jumped to my feet. Bending, I grabbed my discarded clothes and rushed from the room as my entire body heated from embarrassment.

CHAPTER SEVENTEEN
LORCAN

S LEDGE MARCHED INTO THE house the second Pepper slammed her bedroom door shut. His expression made me jump to my feet and hold up my hands in a placating manner.

"I told you not to fool around with Pepper," he said, pacing the room while clenching and unclenching his hands.

"I—"

"Nothing you say can make it all right. You're making her another notch in your long line of women."

There was only one sentence I could say to shut him up, and that was telling him the truth. Pepper wasn't another woman. She was the woman. My fated mate. The moment her lips landed on mine I'd known Rian was right and I'd ignored the signs Pepper was destined to be mine. If I told him, Sledge would expect me to claim her and let her into my heart. I wouldn't subject her to the dark stain inside me. She was too beautiful to have my darkness.

Sledge continued his rant, and I stood there taking everything he said. He was right. I shouldn't have touched her, but now I had, there was no way I'd take it back. There was no way I'd stop myself from touching her again. She was like a temptation I didn't want to resist.

Pepper walked back into the room. Her long hair was damp, and a fresh set of clothes hugged her body. A body I'd become very intimate with a moment ago. My cock jumped at the sight of her. If not for Sledge, then I would have buried myself inside her damp heat and lost myself to the pleasure of my mate.

"Cut it out, Sledge," Pepper said. "I'm twenty-eight years old and Lorcan did nothing I didn't want him to do."

"He's three hundred and twenty-two years old." Sledge stopped pacing to face her.

"Really?" Her eyes widened and her eyebrows shot into her hairline.

Pepper appeared rattled by my age, but she recovered her surprise by saying, "Of course, he's older. He's a Fae. I bet Briana is older than you."

Sledge huffed. "You don't understand what he's like."

"And you do?" She cocked her hip.

My mind dived to the way she'd enjoyed my lips on her hip. Why couldn't I stay focused on the conversation? Come to my mate's defense at least.

"I witnessed Briana's memories. I see him better than you do."

"So what?" She shrugged. "If I want to have fun with Lorcan, I will."

"Damn it, Pepper, you're family, part of my pack, I need to protect you from getting hurt."

Pepper's expression morphed into one of softness.

"I'm part of your pack?"

"Of course." Sledge nodded.

"But I'm not a wolf shifter."

"It doesn't matter. You have shifter blood in your veins. You are pack and we look after our pack members."

Pepper's eyes glistened. Was she about to cry? Did Sledge claiming her as a pack member mean that much to her? She threw her arms around Sledge and hugged him. He grunted in surprise but returned her embrace with his thick arms around her smaller frame. They reminded me so much of my brother and sisters and how we bickered yet protected each other.

He patted the top of her head. She shook him off with a fake glare if I'd ever seen one.

"I want to talk to Lorcan. Can you give us space?"

"Sure. I'll be in the kitchen making dinner."

"Eavesdropping?" Pepper asked.

"I can't help my powerful hearing."

"You can leave," she pointed out.

"Then dinner would be late."

I almost laughed at their exchange.

Pepper waved her hand toward the kitchen. "Don't blame me if you hear something you don't like."

Sledge shrugged his massive shoulders and left the room. Pepper walked closer to me until she was within embracing distance, but I didn't take her into my arms like I wanted. She tilted her head and ran her gaze over my face.

"I can't tell what you're thinking," she said. "Before I could, but not now."

I stayed quiet within the mask I'd plastered on my face. If I let my emotions show, she'd see every fear I had inside me. She'd know how much she meant to me. How much I longed to claim her as my fated mate.

"Do you regret what we did?" she asked.

I scowled. "I'd never regret bringing you to orgasm."

"But you regretted something. I saw it on your face."

She was too observant for me to deny I had regrets. About how I couldn't truly make her mine in the way of the Fae.

"I regretted Sledge interrupting us."

She dropped her gaze to her feet, which were bare like mine. Fae never wore shoes because the powerful vibrations coming from the earth fed into our magic. Witches practiced organic magic too. Did she sense the magic beneath the soles of her feet? She'd worn black boots earlier today. I longed to take her outside and ask her if the earth fed the magic she could control.

"I don't think that's the only thing you regret."

Did she have even more wolf-shifter blood than she said? Could she hear the small omission from my statement?

"Pepper," I said, gathering her hands in mine. "I don't regret kissing you. I don't regret touching you. So never think that."

"I'm not sure what to think. A lot happened this afternoon." She wriggled her hands out of my grasp.

I let her go. Whatever my mate needed, I'd give it to her. She picked up the discarded grimoire and ran a hand over the etched willow tree on the leather cover.

"I understand."

"You do?" She placed the book on the table.

"Aye. You don't have to worry about me touching you again."

"Wait. That's not what I meant."

"What do you want then?" I asked, trying not to keep the hopeful note out of my voice. I wanted her to choose me, but I wanted her to tell me to leave her alone too. If she did, then I wouldn't have to battle with the dilemma to tell her she was my fated mate. It would be impossible for me to place a Fae mating mark on her. She'd either end up in a lifelong coma or die if I did.

"Well," she said, stepping closer once again. "I want another of those orgasms you gave me."

A loud clatter of pans fell to the floor in the kitchen. Served Sledge right for eavesdropping. I laughed and met the distance Pepper was intent on closing between us.

"I'm sure I can do that again."

She lifted her hands to my chest and placed a palm over my heart. Did witches have a mating mark similar to the Fae? Was she about to claim me? But she didn't realize she was my fated mate. Every ounce of my power throbbed in anticipation. My hands glowed as my power longed to place my mark on her.

I cupped her backside and hauled her against my body. She gasped as she rubbed against my throbbing erection, which hadn't gone down since the second her lips touched mine.

"So, you're old?" She cocked an eyebrow.

"I suppose I am compared to you."

"And you learned all your skills in bed with many women?"

"Aye."

"I can't blame them. You're very hot." She ran her hands up to my shoulders.

I laughed.

"How many?"

My laughter snapped off. "A lot."

"I'm no virgin either." Her fingers stroked the back of my neck.

"I couldn't tell." To stop myself from laughing, I pressed my lips together.

She flicked my ear with her fingers and pretended to be annoyed. All this time she'd been so standoffish with everyone when it was a pretense. She wasn't that way. She was warm and caring. Pepper wanted to be loved.

I wanted to be the one to love her.

And I would. She was fated for me, and I'd stay by her side for the rest of her life. I'd watch her age and die for witches were mortal.

I kissed her before the dark thoughts about her death swamped me and dragged me into a deep pit. Pepper melted into my body as though made for me and me alone. She was, but she didn't comprehend the depth of our connection. The absolute dedication of a fated mate. The love I'd form for her from this day forward.

"Dinner is ready," Sledge called from the kitchen.

CHAPTER EIGHTEEN
PEPPER

D INNER HAD BEEN QUIET and awkward with Sledge shooting annoyed looks at Lorcan. Lorcan smirked in his too-devastating way, which sent my heart and body into overdrive. I dashed from the room the second I'd finished my plate. Sledge wasn't the best cook, but I wouldn't hurt his feelings. After the way he'd gone all big brother protective of me, I'd opened a small part of me into believing I was part of his pack. Is this what a genuine family was like? I grabbed my family grimoire and shut myself in my bedroom. Sledge's and Lorcan's voices were a distant muffled sound in the otherwise quiet hotel.

With reverence, I flicked open the first page. The scrawling black script writing was bold, a lot like the legends of Saltine.

The book of Woodswillow.

Woodswillow was our original surname, but they had shortened it somewhere along the line to Willow. I preferred Woodswillow. It had a more magical sound to it. I traced my finger over the lettering. A surge of magic zapped the tip of my finger.

Holy moly, this book had a lot of magic and that was even before I'd read the spells and potion recipes. I leaned down and inhaled, drawing in the scent of old pages and Lorcan. He'd imbedded his scent in this book. He'd had this grimoire in his possession for centuries. Why would Saltine entrust a Fae to hold our family's legacy? It made little sense. Unless there was something Lorcan wasn't telling me about the night Saltine gave him the grimoire.

I flicked to the first page of the book. A picture accompanied a truth spell and all the variations of the potion one might ever need for every different supernatural creature. I let out a cackle. I could have used this earlier. If I had, then Eloise would still be alive to question further, not that I considered she had anything useful to add.

Lighting candles around the room, I settled in the middle of the bed to read the book from start to finish. It might take me all night, or a couple of nights even, with how thick it was, but I hungered to learn every detail of my family, every spell, every potion.

A dark shadow lurched toward me. Rotten hands outstretched as though ready to grab my throat and choke the life from my body. My mouth wouldn't open.

The scream stuck inside. Flesh fell from the fingers in thick goblets landing on the floor with a wet thud. The hands kept coming closer until the bleeding, decayed flesh touched mine.

Silent screams echoed inside my head.

No part of my body would move to ward off the attack. My mouth wouldn't say the protection spell repeating inside my mind. The one from my family grimoire. The new spell wouldn't stop with the incessant words. So much so that I believed it might drive me insane before the hideous hands choked the life from me.

Orange flames flickered to life. A wall of fire raced toward me so fast. The heat from the inferno was so hot sweat dripped into my eyes and all the while the hands kept strangling me.

"Pepper, wake up," Lorcan's voice echoed as if it came from a great distance.

I wanted to call for his help, but I still couldn't move. I could no longer breathe with the hands closing around my neck and the fire stripping the air of oxygen. Death was coming for me.

"Pepper," Lorcan called louder this time.

I focused on his voice, the command in his tone, the pleading that did things to my heart, instead of the spell chanting inside my mind.

"Pepper, wake up now, dammit."

My eyes snapped open. Worried frown lines creased Lorcan's face.

"Thank, Dia." His shoulders sagged.

I gawked around the room but there were no monster hands or wall of flames. No death waiting for me. Only Lorcan.

"What happened?" I asked through a mouth devoid of moisture.

"You had a bad dream again."

"Oh." I placed a shaky hand on my throat expecting it to be tender, as though the hands strangling me had been real, but my neck was fine under my probing fingers.

"Can you remember what it was about?" he asked, stroking my damp hair away from my face.

"Monsters and fire." I shuddered. "Just a crazy nightmare."

Or was it?

Lorcan's frown deepened until I pondered he might end up with permanent lines. Was that possible for a Fae? He looked like a healthy, very fit, young man.

He dangled a small pouch from his fingers. "Try this under your pillow."

I touched the fabric, and the scent of lavender filled the space between us.

"You made me a dream pillow?"

"Aye." He leaned forward and tucked the small object under my pillow.

He was so sweet to make something to ward off my bad dreams. Who was Lorcan under all the hostility he'd portrayed in the beginning? I found I hungered to learn everything about him. I curled my hand into the back of his neck and lifted my head, kissing him on the lips.

His breath rushed out of him as he fell into the kiss with enthusiasm. We kissed for an eternity. Each stroke of his talented tongue chased away the remnants of the nightmare and ignited my arousal.

"Pepper." He groaned, kissing his way down my neck.

I urged him on with my fingers. He inspired greedy moans from my mouth. A longing for lust and maybe a little love.

"Keep going," I urged him.

His warm breath brushed over the damp skin on my neck from his ravenous kisses. Goose bumps rippled over my body.

"Every time you kiss me, I can't stop."

"I'll have to remember that," I said.

He chuckled and ripped my panties free with a loud tear of the fabric as though he was more impatient than me at this moment.

I gasped, but his warm mouth descended between my legs and his tongue licked my eager flesh. Last time he'd taken forever to touch me intimately, but this time he dove into my core with his tongue like he wanted to brand me from the inside out. His tongue slipped in and out of me and it was so good all I was capable of was keeping still and panting while he fucked me with his tongue.

"Lorcan," I moaned, gripping the sheets in my hands.

He hummed, sending vibrations through his tongue and lips and making every muscle in my core contract then explode into a powerful orgasm. My entire body quivered as wave after wave of pleasure rushed through me. Lorcan lifted his head and studied me yet again in the throes of ecstasy. Each contraction of my orgasm, while pleasurable, was empty without him inside me.

"Holy moly." I dropped my head back on the pillow. "I've never come so quick in my life."

"It's no wonder. You've had such a brief life."

I sat up and reached for the buttons on his shirt.

"What are you doing?" he asked.

"Getting you naked." I stopped unbuttoning his shirt to lift my singlet over my head. "Like I am."

His gaze heated with so much lust a fresh pool of liquid arousal coated me.

"Can't I please you?"

I cupped his massive erection through his pants and rubbed my hand up and down, imagining the way he'd slide inside me. His thick length would feel so good, but I wanted to make him feel as good as he'd made me.

"Or you can let me please you too."

CHAPTER NINETEEN
LORCAN

D IA. IS THIS WHAT having a fated mate felt like? I'd fallen into a new utopia. One where my mate wanted to satisfy me and not expect anything in return. I couldn't stop her touching me even if I wanted to, and I didn't. I longed to have her touch me day and night for eternity. My eyes wanted to close, but I kept them open because watching her face was my new favorite pastime.

Her fingers returned to my shirt buttons, and she slid them free. Pushing my shirt from my shoulders she ran her hands up my forearms, over my biceps, and across my chest.

"I could tell you had muscles hidden under those princely clothes," she said.

I smirked. Many hours of training with the guards had honed my body into a solid mass of muscle. Women always commented on my form, but none had ever mattered until Pepper. The words from her lips made me feel cockier than I ever had in my long life.

"You like my muscles?" I lifted my arms and flexed my biceps.

Pepper laughed and placed her hands on them. I kept flexing them, so she felt the muscles moving beneath her palms. She stopped laughing and dropped her hands into my pants.

"I think I'll like this muscle the most."

I laughed at her sassiness, but I cut it short when she opened my pants and slid her warm palm around my aching length. Dia, her touch was insane. I'd never experienced such pleasure from a simple act before but with my fated mate, everything was more intense. More pleasurable. Wringing orgasms from her pleased me more than anything in my life. Once she brought me to orgasm, then I'd never let her go.

She lifted her other hand to her mouth and swiped her tongue along her palm all while watching me with a smirk that might have mirrored my earlier expression. She switched hands and glided her moist palm along my cock until every stroke had me fighting to hold back an orgasm. I wouldn't come as quickly as her. I wanted to make her come more before she gave me the ecstasy hanging at the edges of my control.

"Problem?" She raised an eyebrow with a knowing smirk.

"No," I croaked.

"Then let me keep playing." She wriggled her arm.

"But I want to make you come again."

"And I want to make you come."

A smile tugged at my lips. She might have been obedient earlier, but I didn't expect her to want to be in charge. I preferred being in charge. If I let my control go, then I might mark her on accident. No. I had to stay in charge. I had to keep her safe even from me.

"Put your mouth on me."

She let go as though my command was what she wanted all along. She released my cock from her tight grip and replaced it with the blissful warm haven of her mouth. I placed a hand on the back of her head and held her still.

"Now don't move."

She mumbled something, but it was so low and husky I couldn't decipher her words.

I stroked my other hand toward her breasts and played with her nipples. Soft strokes at first making her moan around my cock in her mouth. Then tugs on her nipples making her squeak. Each little sound sent a new vibration through my cock. I tugged and stroked until I thought she'd make me come just from the sounds coming from her.

Almost at the edge of my control, I dipped my hand between her legs. Her slick arousal met my fingers, and a new moan took up residence in her throat. Each slide of my fingers over her flesh made her dip her head a fraction lower as though she wanted to swallow me down the back of her throat. The sensitive tip of my cock hit the back of her throat and my fingers tightened in her hair. She shivered and more moisture gushed onto my fingers. I slid them inside her and she came with a long-drawn-out moan over my cock. My cock swelled to the point of no return, and I tugged her head away, flipped her onto her back, and buried myself into her still-quivering flesh.

The look of rapt pleasure on her face almost made me lose control. My palms flared with my power, lighting up the room into a blueish-green tinge adding to the magic of the moment.

"Fuck, Lorcan," she said with a breathy sigh.

"Yes, you will." I rolled my hips forward.

She gasped as my cock massaged her oversensitive flesh. The connection from being inside her almost took all my control. My fated mate eager for me made my cock throb painfully to give her what she wanted. She lifted her feet and hooked them around my hips. The new angle drove me deeper with each thrust setting a streak of pleasure running down the back of my spine. She held my bulging biceps as though they would stop her from shifting up the bed, but each time I buried myself to the hilt, her body moved until her head touched the headboard. She lifted her hands behind her head and arched her back. Dia, she was perfect.

Unable to give into the temptation of her exposed breasts, I lowered my mouth to her nipple and rolled it between my teeth. She let out a breathy moan and rocked her hips in time with mine. On and on we moved in sync. Magical. Timeless. Exquisite pleasure. My balls drew up tight. My cock surged with every thrust begging me to let go. Give in to the ultimate pleasure awaiting me. The pleasure of my fated mate.

Her body trembled underneath mine as though she too experienced this soul-rendering moment of the connection of fated mates. Her legs tightened in a vice-like grip. Sensing she was nearing another orgasm, I lifted my head to watch the rapture light up her face. I could watch her every minute of every day like this. The next roll of my hips gave me what I wanted. Pepper's breath stuttered as she came on my cock. The moment was suspended in time as though we were the only two in existence. Her inner muscles clamped around me like a perfect dream and I had no choice but to follow her into the blissful freefall. The most powerful orgasm of my existence rushed through my body. My power surged so much to my hands that I had to force them to the side of the mattress instead of on Pepper's chest where the magical urge wanted me to put them. To sear my mating mark in her chest. Share with her my most intimate memories. Let her love me as I would love her.

Every contracting ripple of her orgasm made mine intensify as time snapped back into existence. She squeezed my cock in a grip of ecstasy, one I never wanted to leave. Her eyes locked on my face as though she too wanted to watch the thrall roll over my expression.

And she enthralled me.

Downright captivated by the witch who was my fated mate.

If only I could place a Fae mate mark on her chest.

CHAPTER TWENTY

PEPPER

THE BEST SEX OF my life. Hell, it'd perhaps stay that way for the rest of my life. No one would compete with the way we'd connected right now. I slid my hands to Lorcan's neck and lifted my head into the crook of his shoulder. His arms slid around my back and a different tingle coated my skin. I vaguely remembered his power lighting up his hands. I guess this was what it was like to be touched by him when his hands were aglow with magic. It was a unique pleasure, but still arousing.

Lorcan rolled us on the bed until he cradled me to his chest. The embrace was sweet. Comforting. All the things I'd never have expected from him, but it felt right like this was where I was meant to be. I wasn't sure what to say since he'd simply come in here to wake me from a bad dream, and I'd seduced him.

"Are you always quiet after sex?" he asked.

"No," I mumbled into his chest.

"Do you want me to leave?"

"No," I said without even having to think why.

Silence descended between us again. I sensed Lorcan's unease by the way his muscles were tense underneath me, but what might I say? We'd almost hated each other and now we'd... dare I think it... made love?

"What is bothering you then?"

"I'm not sure," I lied.

I'd wanted to experience what it'd be like with Lorcan, but I'd never expected to develop feelings for the Fae Prince from sex. How could I have feelings for him? I barely knew the man.

Lorcan's hands stopped glowing, plunging the room into the softer glow of the candlelight. I sighed and rolled over.

"Do you think Sledge overheard us?"

Lorcan chuckled. "Probably most of the town did. They're all wolf shifters."

"Shit." I slapped my hand over my face.

He tugged it free and peered into my eyes. "If it bothers you that much then next time, I'll take you somewhere else."

"Next time?" I asked.

"Aye." He placed a tender kiss on my lips. "Many times."

"Oh. Okay."

He laid his head on the pillow beside mine and I snuggled back into his welcoming arms. We lay cuddled together for a long time simply holding each other. More emotions welled inside my heart. If he was simply here for sex, wouldn't he have run back to his room by now?

Did Lorcan want me as much as I wanted the connection with him?

"Did you find anything of use in your grimoire?" he asked, breaking through the questions running rampant inside my head.

I sat up and grabbed the book Lorcan must have placed on the bedside table because I didn't remember doing that before I fell asleep.

"There is a lot in here. Saltine and her family before her comprehended a lot about the supernatural creatures."

"She did. I've read your grimoire many times over the years wondering why she tasked me with its care. It contains a large amount of information and spells and potions. A great deal more than the one you stole."

I flipped open the book. "This spell here will work on the rock. I'll need to gather ingredients first though."

"We can do that tomorrow. I've visited a few places where certain herbs grow."

"No need. I have a special herb garden at my house. I'll head there tomorrow and collect what I need and fly back. It'll take me a few days with all the travel."

"Where do you live?"

"I have a small cottage in England."

"A few days is too long."

"Unless Sledge has an herb garden, then that's the fastest way to find mandrake root."

Lorcan frowned. "Mandrake root is dangerous. I'll find it for you."

"Do you even know where to look?"

"Tell me where you live, and I'll cross through the Veil and fetch it."

"No way. I'm not telling you where I live."

"Why not?" He huffed. "Don't you trust me?"

"No one knows where I live, and I'd like to keep it that way."

"You're so infuriating." He stood and dressed, his movements jerky as though I'd angered him.

He didn't understand what it was like being a witch though. People sought us out for our spells and potions but if they didn't work the way they desired, then they were angry and often wanted their money back. Some people were even violent about it. I'd learned that lesson the hard way.

"I don't want to wind up murdered like my parents," I yelled.

Lorcan froze like a statue as if any movement would crack him into a thousand pieces. His hands lit up like they were out of control with power. Time ticked, and he still didn't move.

"Lorcan?" I whispered, afraid I'd break him if I spoke too loudly.

He breathed through his mouth in long drawn-out breaths.

"Who killed them?" he ground out through clenched teeth. "I'll find them and kill them for you."

I dropped the book and scrambled before him to peer into his eyes. The cold calculating stare of death made my body tremble.

"You don't need to kill anyone for me."

"But they hurt your parents."

"They did, but karma will catch up with them if it hasn't already."

He flung his glowing hands up in the air. "How can you not want revenge?"

"I did. For a long time. I contemplated hexing them or cursing them, but I became so focused on my rage that it consumed me. I didn't like the person I was turning into, so I let it go. As much as I want whoever killed my parents to suffer, I don't want to be the one to cause it. We have a saying in the covens that once we use our magic for evil, we turn evil ourselves. I don't know if it's true, but the way I was feeling..." I swallowed back the way those feelings of evil had consumed me. "I don't want to be evil."

His hands stopped glowing, and he stepped toward the French door leading outside.

"You'd never be evil."

"You can't know that."

"I can since I'm way older than you."

His teasing tone made me laugh.

"All right, so tomorrow you'll fly home unless I find mandrake root first." He opened the door and stepped outside.

A cool breeze gusted into the room and blew out the candles, but outside the area around Lorcan lit up in a glowing blue-green mist. Magic swirled and intensified. The particles vibrated through the air making every hair in my body stand on end. Lorcan stepped into the glowing Veil and disappeared.

"Holy moly," I muttered under my breath. "How powerful is he?"

CHAPTER TWENTY-ONE

LORCAN

A FTER A QUICK TRIP back to the Summer Court, I put in an appearance with the family, talking with them and acting like nothing was wrong, which was harder than I assumed. What was even harder, was being away from Pepper. The pull toward my fated mate was intense. All the time, my palms wanted to glow and mark her in the way of the Fae. Every fiber in my being wanted to return to Earth. Return to Pepper. Never leave her side.

Aislinn joined me on the side of the ballroom where refreshments lined a table for the guests. I'd escaped a flirtatious Fae woman wanting to dance with me saying I needed refreshments. Before Pepper, I would have taken her up on the offer for the dance and more, but now, other women repulsed me. The notion of having another woman touch me made me feel ill inside my stomach.

My sister filled a goblet with a delicious mixture of fruit juices, which I was already sipping. I'd talked with

Briana and made sure she stayed in the Summer Court with Saoirse, making it sound as though Saoirse wanted her there. As long as everyone stayed here then I didn't care what lies I told.

I was as bad as Father.

Aislinn sipped her drink and eyed me over the rim of the goblet.

"What?" I asked.

"You're up to something."

I lifted my goblet. "Drinking?"

"No." She sidestepped closer to me and lowered her voice. "What is it?"

"What are you talking about?"

"Cut the shite, Lorcan. Mother and Father tasked me to keep you and Saoirse out of trouble when you were younger. I've seen the look on your face before and understand what it means even if no one else does. You're up to something."

Trust my older sister to call me out. She never could just let me be.

"I met a woman on Earth and I'm courting her."

Her eyes narrowed. She without a doubt didn't believe me. I had a lot of Fae women in the Summer Court waiting for me to court them. I didn't need to go to Earth for women. One woman though... my fated mate was a different matter.

"What is she?"

Shite.

I tugged on the collar of my shirt. "Does it matter?"

"If you're skulking around, then it does."

My lips firmed into a tight line. Here was the other reason I was worried about Pepper being my fated mate. What if my family despised witches as I had for the role they'd played in our massacre? Had? Wait. Did I no longer despise them? My stomach flipped in a somersault. No, I didn't. When had that happened?

"I believed it mattered, but I'm no longer sure it does. She's a witch."

"Shite," Aislinn said blowing out the word in a long breath.

"I acted that way too. I despised her the moment I met her for the past, but I was wrong to do so."

"Lorcan." She slammed her goblet on the table. "This is wrong. Fooling around with the Fae women is one thing but fooling around with a witch is different."

"I'm not fooling around with her. She's my fated mate."

She grabbed my arms. "Are you making a joke?"

"No."

Her face twisted into horror and disgust.

"We don't choose our fated mate so don't give me the high and mighty look. Wait until fate sends you your mate, then we'll see who he is."

Her eyes glistened as though she was about to cry. Aislinn cry? Never. What had I said to upset her?

She released my arms. "I hope for your sake you're wrong."

"Why?"

"How do you think Mother and Father will take the news?"

I'd deliberated about them. Many times. Father used to visit Saltine a lot so he might accept a witch from her family line as my fated mate. After all, Saltine had helped us destroy the Trappers.

"I think they'll be fine with it."

"What aren't you telling me?"

"I can ask you the same question." I stepped closer to her and lowered my voice. "Aislinn, why won't you tell me what happened that night I rescued you? One minute I was untying you from the stake, the next second there was a bright flash and you'd vanished in front of my eyes. I was frantic with worry searching for you, and when I found you—"

"I was crying," she finished for me.

"Why were you crying?"

"I was in pain. They'd burned my feet."

"But how did you vanish? Why were you beside the cottage? How did you get there?"

"I've told you before, I don't remember." Her lips formed into a tight line.

"I don't believe you and I don't know why you won't tell me what happened to you during that time. You know I'd hurt anyone who hurt you."

"I know, Lorcan. I'm glad you found me for the second time that night and I'm glad you didn't tell anyone I'd disappeared for a moment."

"Aislinn, whatever happened, I want to help."

"You can't help. No one can."

She huffed and stomped away. Aislinn turned as she reached the edge of the ballroom and gave me one last stare. Whatever else had happened to her that night, it had to have been bad for her to keep it a secret all these centuries. I'd tried many times to get answers from her, but every time she said she didn't remember. I didn't believe her though, because she'd changed so much after that night. Maybe when she found her fated mate, and she shared it with him during the marking he'd understand her. Then she'd understand I'd had no choice in who my fated was as well.

"What did you say to Aislinn?" Roisin asked, gliding over to me so majestically her gown appeared to float across the goldstone flooring in the ballroom.

I shrugged. Aislinn wanted her secrets kept, and I'd kept them for her this long. I wouldn't break her confidence now.

Plus Roisin was the baby of the family even though she hated us treating her that way.

"She's been teaching me her throwing knives."

"Dia, be careful."

Roisin laughed. "They're fun and I've only cut my fingers a few times."

I opened my mouth to tell her to be more careful, but I snapped it shut. She was immortal, a few knicks from throwing knives wouldn't kill her, but the protective urge surged. Roisin was my sister, and I didn't want her to get hurt. No wonder Sledge was so annoyed about me being with Pepper. Perhaps when I returned, I'd put his mind to rest that I wouldn't hurt her because she was my fated mate. I'd cherish her and worship her for as long as she lived.

"I'm heading up to my room for a nap," I said and kissed her cheek.

"Nap?" She laughed.

"I'll be back later."

Even my youngest sister perceived my promiscuity.

For the first time, I dreaded revealing how many lovers I'd had to Pepper even though she'd seemed to take the news well before. I strode from the ballroom and ducked into the atrium. Of course, I wasn't alone. Mother sat on a boulder with Ailbhe in her arms.

"Are you showing the young prince our spring?"

"Aye. He loves it here," Mother said.

Ailbhe chatted in his baby language. Fireflies flitted through the open ceiling and danced. I was glad they were bonding, but I needed them to leave so I could slip through the Veil undetected from the place with the strongest connection to our powers.

"Saoirse was looking for you," I lied.

"She was?" Mother frowned, but stood and hoisted Ailbhe onto her hip.

Grandmotherhood suited her. She smiled wider than I'd seen in a long time. She left the atrium, and I didn't waste time using my royal powers to unlock the Veil. I slipped inside the glowing mist and closed it behind me. Now to find mandrake root. Where could I search? Earth was enormous. It might be anywhere. It was a witch ingredient so the best place to look would be with a witch, but I wasn't friends with any witch. The only place I considered was Saltine's old house, which was reduced to ruins, but if the garden was still intact...

My thoughts took me to my destination. I stepped out of the Veil. A bubbling brook gurgled beside me. Weeping willows lined the creek. Their leaves hung like long fingers trying to touch me. I walked the dirt path as I had all those years ago. So many memories assaulted me all at once it threatened to overwhelm me. My knees shook. A lump formed in my throat. Flashes of red fire burned behind my eyelids. Pain and suffering churned my stomach. My power sought an outlet for the emotions overwhelming me. The night I'd lost family and friends. The night I'd become a killer. I lifted my glowing hands to the sky and shot a bolt of lightning. The tension eased with the surge of power. My lungs eased, and the pain lessened. I shoved the memories into the dark crevice of my mind and continued along the path.

My feet skidded to a halt. Where I'd expected to see the ruins of Saltine's house, stood a cottage of white brick and a thatched roof. Had it repaired itself with magic? Was that even possible? There were minor differences between the former house and the new house and the surrounding garden, but it was similar enough to remind me of Saltine even after not laying eyes on it for centuries.

I walked toward the low white picket fence and gate half expecting Saltine to open the door and stride out with her eerie cackle. When that didn't happen, I breathed a sigh. How could she be alive after all this time? Witches were mortal. I opened the gate and walked up to the door and knocked. No one answered, and I listened for a long time trying to decipher if anyone was home. When no sounds came, I faced her garden.

It would have been easier to go inside and hope whoever lived here had mandrake root already on their shelf, but I wouldn't break into someone's home. The garden was free pickings though. I strode through the plants looking for the long green leaves of the mandrake. After a long search, I found it. Kneeling beside the plant, I wished I'd brought an offering with me as I didn't want the plant to scream when I harvested it. Nor did I want it to kill me.

The power of the earth called to me, and I placed my hands on the soil beside the mandrake to send my power deep into the soil. Around me, all the plants surged as though they'd received a dose of fertilizer.

"I offer my power to your neighbors so they may flourish in exchange for your roots."

I sent another surge of power into the plants and hoped my offering was enough. With my fingers, I dug the top of the soil away from the roots exposing what I needed for Pepper. If it aimed to kill me, so be it, I'd do anything for my mate. I gripped the root and held my breath waiting for the murderous scream. When none came, I yanked the mandrake root from the soil.

Out came the twisted form of the mandrake root.

A laugh burst free unheeded.

In my palm lay the distinct shape of a penis.

CHAPTER TWENTY-TWO

PEPPER

T HE NIGHT AIR BRUSHED across my face like the cool fingers of Mother Nature herself as I strode around the back garden of the hotel. Who did Lorcan think he was disappearing like that? Oh, so what if he was a Fae Prince, and that was his normal way of travel? After I'd said I'd harvest the mandrake root myself, why did he have to rush off all knight in shining armor? The idiot didn't realize I'd been harvesting the root since I was a child. The coven taught all witches how to harvest herbs. It was the first thing we learned before spells and potions.

A firefly buzzed around my head making me go cross-eyed as it landed on the tip of my nose.

Lorcan's laughter echoed around the garden. The Veil swirled into existence. No, that wasn't right, it always existed, I just couldn't see it. He stepped from the magical mist and closed it behind him. I flapped my hand to shoo away the firefly, but it was like the damn thing was stuck to my nose. Lorcan lifted his glowing hand,

and the bug flew toward him, landing on the tip of his finger. It flapped its wings as though telling Lorcan a story, then it flew into the night sky, the twinkling light fading into the distance.

"Where did you go?" I asked.

"To get a mandrake root." He shrugged like it was no big deal.

It was. The mandrake was notorious for being sensitive. Prone to murder its harvester. A tight band constricted around my chest. The notion of Lorcan dying made every bone in my body ache. Made my heart crumble into small pieces as though I wouldn't be whole without him. It was as though magic had connected us in the way others marked their fated mates. Witches didn't have that magic in them, so we didn't have fated mates. We possessed no way to mark a man as ours. To let them and everyone know that their heart and body belonged to someone. I longed for Lorcan to belong to me.

"Gah." I threw my hands up in the air.

Why was I acting so insane?

"Do you have no regard for your life?" I asked.

"Of course, I do."

"Then why would you harvest the mandrake root when I'd have done it?"

"It's okay for you to put your life on the line for a plant and not me?"

We glared at each other. He had a point, but his life was worth more than mine. He was a rare Fae with exceptional powers.

"There are plenty of other witches. How many Fae Princes are there?"

"Two, three now with Saoirse's baby, but that's beside the point."

"No, it's not." I shook my head. "You're special, Lorcan. Your powers are special. We can't lose them."

"I'm not special."

It was his turn to shake his head.

"How can you say that?" I pointed at his glowing hands. "You don't see my hands glowing."

His lips twitched like he wanted to smile.

"You haven't even seen me use my powers in their entirety." He smirked.

"For the best since a killer is hunting you when you use them."

Lorcan jolted to alert and searched the surrounding area as though the killer would attack now.

"Once I kill him, I'll show you all the magic you want to see."

"Promise?" I asked.

"I promise."

"Good," I said, stepping closer.

"You're special too," Lorcan said.

My lips parted, but he placed a hand over my mouth silencing any protest I might make.

"There might be plenty of other witches but there's only one witch for me and that's you."

The way he talked to me twined my heart into believing he wanted me forever. It was a heady feeling to have a Fae prince desire you. I fisted his shirt and tugged him toward me. His hand fell away a second before our lips met. He kissed me as though he meant every word. I'd meant every one of mine. Lorcan was special to his people as their prince. He was special to me too. The infuriating handsome Fae had love-struck me.

So much so my heart would soon be his and his alone. If we didn't kill each other first.

"You shouldn't have kissed me," he said.

"What? Why?" I gasped.

"Because I won't stop now until we're both satisfied."

"I don't see a problem with that."

I slid my hand into his pants and froze. Did he have two cocks now?

Lorcan threw back his head and laughed as he slid his hand into his pocket and drew out the mandrake root. I slapped his chest in a playful tiny touch.

His laughter continued. "Your face was priceless."

"Yeah... well," I stuttered.

He laughed harder. "Disappointed it wasn't another cock in my pants?"

I snorted. "No."

"Liar," he said, placing his lips on the shell of my ear. "You'd take two of me."

"One is more than enough." I cupped him through his pants, then I raised an eyebrow. "Although can you make two with your powers?"

"Witch," he said, "you'd be more liable out of the two of us to come up with magic for that."

I pursed my lips and considered it. Would it be possible? Could I come up with a new spell to have him with two cocks? How many people would buy that spell? A damn lot probably.

"Pepper," he said, sliding his hand into my pants. "Stop thinking about ways to grow more cocks and do something with the one in your hand."

I laughed and slid my hand inside his pants, grasping the firm length of his hardness and groaning at the silken magical sensation running over my palm. His lips landed on mine in another soul-shattering kiss. The way his tongue caressed mine made me frantic for more. Lorcan's hand glowed and slid inside my pants. I gasped at the way he lit me up from the contact of his powers on my most sensitive flesh.

"A little touch," he said, lowering me to the ground.

The night sky surged with twinkling stars behind his head. Beneath my back, the soft blanket of grass beneath us grew thicker and lusher. The serenade of the night creatures crooned to us as if by magic. Was Lorcan's power at play in making this night even more spectacular than it was? He stripped my clothes from my body and whispered how beautiful I was with each touch of his fingers and lips. Lorcan made me feel every bit as special as he said I was. Even under the cool breeze, our skin heated until we were both sweaty with passion. Until we both lost ourselves in the euphoria of each other's bodies. Every second with Lorcan made me fall even deeper under his spell. I never wanted this night to end.

CHAPTER TWENTY-THREE
PEPPER

LORCAN AND I MUST have dozed off naked under the stars because the sun rising and glaring in my face woke me. I sat up with a start and scrambled for my clothes before Sledge woke and glanced out of a window. I didn't want my relative to see me naked. Witches didn't run around naked like wolf shifters. I guess they usually had fur covering their bodies though. Lorcan roused with my harried rustling and sat up with a self-satisfied smirk. He lifted the penis-shaped mandrake root and waggled his eyebrows.

I tossed his shirt in his direction. He laughed as it hit him in the face.

"I can't remember the last time I laughed this much."

"Glad I amuse you." I stood, yanking on my pants.

Lorcan stretched, sending his muscles rippling and making me pause a moment in distraction. He stood and dressed in an unhurried manner. I sighed, wanting him all over again even though he'd given me many orgasms yesterday. They didn't feel like they were enough. My body ached with the need to have his hands on me. Dressed, he lifted his gaze to my face. I took a step toward him unable to stop myself from touching him any longer.

A throat cleared snapping my attention from Lorcan.

"Good morning." Sledge beamed.

My face heated. Oh crap, he would have overheard us all night.

"Sleep well?" Sledge asked with a cocked lift of his eyebrow.

"Quite well," Lorcan said with a decadent stretch.

"Is that a penis in your hand?" Sledge asked.

"It's a mandrake root," I said, snatching it from Lorcan's hand.

"Were you getting kinky?"

"What? No!" My face flamed even harder. "It's for a spell."

"What sort of spell? A sex spell?"

"No." I shoved the mandrake root behind my back.

Lorcan chuckled. "Witches often use mandrake root in love, sex, and fertility spells, so maybe Sledge has a point."

I narrowed my eyes. "It's for protection against evil."

Turning as huffily as possible, I walked into my bedroom and closed the door and the curtain, shutting out the sight of Lorcan and Sledge laughing together. I guess my talk with Sledge changed his attitude toward Lorcan. Setting the mandrake root down on the bedside table, I walked into the bathroom to take a long hot shower and try not to think of Lorcan.

I walked into the kitchen with one arm cradling the Woodswillow grimoire and the other an assortment of herbs. Lorcan and Sledge were seated at the table eating. One whiff of the food had me wrinkling my nose.

"What are you eating?"

Lorcan lifted his spoon and let a stream of runny goo drip from it. "He said porridge."

"It doesn't even smell like it." I swiped the bowls from under them and dumped them in the sink. "Give me five minutes and then you'll have real porridge."

Sledge stretched his arms across the back of the chairs. Lorcan rested his elbows on the table. Were they back to facing each other off?

"So," Sledge said. "Briana, my fated mate, doesn't cook."

Why did he say, fated mate? I appreciated that she was his mate. Lorcan understood she was his mate.

"Why would she?" Lorcan asked. "We have cooks in our palace."

I almost dropped the entire packet of porridge into the saucepan. For some reason, I hadn't even registered Lorcan would live in a palace and have servants. He was a prince for crying out loud. Shaking off how different our lives were even more so than my lack of magic, I added currants to the porridge and stirred the oats until they were thick and creamy. I spooned the porridge into three bowls and added a swirl of honey to the top and a sprinkle of brown sugar.

Lorcan rose and carried the bowls to the table. I searched in the drawers for spoons and carried them and a pitcher of milk to the table.

"You're a terrible host to your guests," I said sitting beside Lorcan.

"You're both family. I don't need to put on a show with you two."

"Good thing you don't need me to leave a review rating," I teased him.

"Such a comedian." He rolled his eyes.

"What is a review rating?" Lorcan asked.

I froze with my spoon on the way to my mouth. Crap, we were from two different worlds altogether and the differences were slapping me in the face left and right this morning.

"It's like guests leaving a comment on their stay for others to read."

"Ah," Lorcan said.

He lifted his spoon and ate the porridge. "This is delicious."

"Thanks." I beamed.

Sledge ate his porridge and grunted to agree with Lorcan. Silence descended as we ate, and it was nice being surrounded by people who cared for me. It'd been so long since I'd had the experience. I'd forgotten how good it was to not be alone. To be in the presence of a dare I say it—family?

When we'd finished, Sledge cleared the bowls and put the dishes in the dishwasher. He kicked the door shut, and said, "Is that the spell for rat rock?"

"Yes."

"Are you and Lorcan planning to explore once you break the spell?"

"Aye," Lorcan said. "If there's a Trapper inside the magical barrier, then once it's down I'll be able to find them and kill them."

"How?" I asked.

"Saltine made a potion, so I'd sense anyone with Trapper blood."

"What if the potion has worn off?" Sledge asked. "You'd be walking into a trap."

Lorcan shrugged as though walking into the face of death was his everyday life. As though chasing a murderer and ending their life was like brushing flint from his clothes. There was a flicker in the depths of his eyes that if I hadn't been so close to him lately, I wouldn't have recognized the shadows.

"The potion wouldn't wear off. It would only end once it fulfilled its purpose. So, if she made the potion for you to track Trappers, then so long as there are Trappers alive, it will be in effect," I said.

Lorcan rubbed his hip. "If I'd known that all those years ago, then I wouldn't have stopped searching when the mark stopped sensing Trappers."

"You have a mark from the potion?"

"Aye." He drew his pants down a fraction and the reddish mark I'd seen on his hip shone in the daylight.

I was too caught up in the pleasure of our bodies to take time and wonder what the mark was, but now I reflected on it, I'd always known there was something magical about it. I'd assumed it was a Fae thing, but this was different.

"Saltine gave you a blood stain." I touched the mark. "We have to get this off you."

"I've had it for centuries. It's no big deal."

"You don't understand. Blood magic is dark magic. There's an element to it that attracts evil. It's why the potion worked. Why you can track the Trappers. You were tracking the evil in them. Sledge grab your largest crock pot and put it on the stove now." I clicked my fingers.

Sensing the urgency in my voice, Sledge jumped into action.

Lorcan placed his hands on my shoulders. "It's no big deal, Pepper."

I placed my hands over his. "Every day that blood magic is in your system, you have an element of evil in you. We need to get it out now before it's too late."

CHAPTER TWENTY-FOUR
LORCAN

I'D READ HER FAMILY grimoire cover to cover many times. It mentioned blood magic but not that it would make me evil.

"Who told you blood magic has an element of evil?"

"The High Priestess, Miss Margo, taught it to our coven."

Who did I believe? Pepper, my fated mate, who was a trained witch? Or the ancient grimoire Saltine tasked to my protection? If Pepper was right, becoming evil was a small price to pay for protecting every Fae.

I'd often wondered about the mark staying on my body, but I'd never imagined it meant a Trapper was still alive. It shouldn't be possible after this long since they were human. But them capturing us shouldn't have been possible to start with.

"Focus on the spell for rat rock," I said.

"But you might turn evil any second."

"Pepper," I soothed. "Another day or two won't make a difference to me when I've had the potion inside me this long."

"You don't know that."

"Perhaps not but finding the Trapper and killing him is the only way to end the potion so stop freaking out."

"Freaking out?" She huffed.

Sledge wisely kept his smart comebacks to himself this time.

I rubbed my thumbs soothingly over the tense muscles in her shoulders. Her fingers dug into mine, stopping my caress.

"Stop trying to distract me with your magic hands."

Sledge choked on a laugh.

I sent a pulse of my power into my hands. Her eyes widened with a surge of desire, but now wasn't the time to get her aroused.

"You're right." I lifted my hands. "I'll stop distracting you, so you can make the potion to break the magical barrier."

"Good," she said, sounding disappointed.

I stepped over to the herbs strewn across the counter. Since she'd been staying here, she'd made the place her home.

"What do you need for the spell?"

"I need you both to get out and let me concentrate." She pointed at the back door.

"Fine by me. Your herbs hurt my nose," Sledge said. "How I'll get the stench out after you're gone is beyond me."

"If you need help, we'll be outside," I said.

Pepper stared at my lips and then sighed. I wanted to kiss her too, but we both knew if we kissed, we wouldn't stop kissing, and kissing would lead to sex.

Sledge opened the back door, and I followed him outside. This side of the house wasn't as pretty as where the hotel rooms opened up to the manicured gardens. It was more rugged and masculine like Sledge. He walked to the furthest corner and inclined his head. I followed him. Sledge sat on a tree stump while I settled leaning against a tree. We stayed that way for a long time until Sledge broke the silence.

"Have you told her?" he asked.

"Told her what?" I frowned.

"Told her she's your fated mate."

"How did you..." I shook my head. Trust everyone to realize who she was to me before I even had. "No. I'm not sure if I'll ever tell her. She wouldn't survive a Fae mating mark."

"Shit. Really?"

"She's mortal."

He glanced toward the kitchen window where we could see Pepper flitting about the kitchen. "But you want to mark her."

"Aye, more than anything."

Sledge grinned, flashing his teeth. "I remember how hard my wolf rode me to mark Briana, but I took my time to overcome her fears first. It worked out best for us that way."

"Pepper isn't afraid of anything."

"I wouldn't say that."

"You've seen her. She's fearless," I said.

"Fearless or thinks she has nothing to lose?"

"I'm finished!" Pepper flung open the back door.

Sledge and I jumped apart like a pair of teenagers caught in a compromising situation.

"Let's go," I said.

Pepper flung her cloak around her shoulders and lifted the hood over her head. Dia, she was beautiful in any clothes and out of them, but the cloak was all her. I understood the way it was a part of her since she'd made it herself with magic. Why couldn't she be immortal? I didn't understand how my fated mate was mortal. Was fate so cruel as to send her to me for such a short time? Pepper strode over to me in her thick boots as though she had a purpose. I almost told her to take the shoes off, so she'd access more power but then remembered she wasn't a Fae. She didn't hold power in her mortal body.

"Do you remember the way?" Sledge asked.

"Yeah." Pepper touched the pouch hanging around her waist.

"Should I come and stand guard or something?" Sledge asked.

"Sure," Pepper said. "Having your muscle nearby couldn't hurt."

A little black box strapped to his belt beeped.

"What's that?" I asked.

"Damn it. It's a fire alert. I can't go with you now." He pulled the small object from his belt and tapped the buttons. "I have to go fight a fire. Some idiot crashed into a tree and the car burst into flames."

"Oh no," Pepper said.

"Wait until I get back," Sledge said.

"No need. One lone Trapper will be easy to dispose of," I said.

"Are you sure?" Sledge asked.

"Aye. He's human and easy to kill."

Sledge frowned but nodded his head. I didn't relish killing another man, but he'd killed first. I was merely stopping him from doing it again.

We walked out of the garden and through the streets of the quaint town. Wolf shifters stared at us, but no one said anything. The stone buildings appeared to be from an older era not as old as me, but older than the cities I'd seen in my travels to Earth. These wolf shifters had a long history here. They were so far from Pepper's home in England that I didn't understand how they were connected.

"How did you discover you and Sledge are related?"

Pepper smiled. "It was pure accident. I was in Australia for a job, and I went to a pub for a drink. Sledge came into the pub with his firefighter team. They were away from Crystal Creek fighting a fire. He took one whiff of me and recognized we were blood kin. We did a bit of digging and discovered one of his relatives mated with Saltine."

"Saltine never had a wolf shifter mate or children when I knew her. She must have lived after that night." My eyebrows rose. "I never thought she'd survive."

"She gave you the family grimoire, so the family tree stopped with her. After we deal with this, I intend to piece it all back together."

"You're hoping to find more of your family?"

"It's a long shot, but there might be more half-witches, half-wolf shifters out there."

"You're not half-wolf shifter though, are you?"

"I suppose not." She shrugged, but it was hard to catch the motion under her cloak. "I'm more witch than anything."

And there lay the problem of me telling her she was my fated mate. If I ever told her, it wouldn't be today anyway, so I pushed the notion aside and concentrated on the problem we faced now. Inside the magical barrier was a Trapper who shouldn't exist. One who didn't look entirely human according to the traitor.

If I killed this Trapper and the blood magic didn't end, then what? Were there more of them alive? Would I become evil as Pepper feared?

CHAPTER TWENTY-FIVE

LORCAN

"**Y**OU FOUND YOUR WAY here with ease," I said, taking in the similar surroundings of the forest. Only someone familiar with the area would recognize where to find the rock. Sledge showing it to Pepper once explained how she recognized the place, but it was like she'd either tracked a scent here or the magic drew her to this place.

If it had been before I'd fallen for Pepper, then I might have said she found her way here with such ease because she recognized where she was going and she was another traitor. I'd never think that now though. I felt like I knew her intimately even though we'd only been together a very short time. Fate accounted for the connection. For the way I'd trust her with anything and everything. Did Pepper sense our bond too? Even as a mortal witch, she must sense there was more between us.

We stopped at the rock that one might say looked like a rat. Roisin, with her artistic eye, would agree.

She would enjoy painting it instead of the roses in the Summer Court. Her paintings overran our rooms, but we had nowhere else to hang them. I'd noted one hanging in Rian and Sophia's treehouse looking so lifelike as all her paintings did one imagined they could touch the softness of the petals. Perhaps there would be more places we'd display her art.

The quiet of the place was eerie. It was as though someone had created a vacuum and sucked the sound from the area around the rock. I didn't like it. Neither did my power. It flickered through my body in waves of overstimulation.

Pepper opened the pouch and fished around inside it. She drew out a long thin bottle that resembled a test tube. The liquid inside shone a luminous green. Unnaturally so. A sense of unease tickled my powers.

"Are you certain you mixed the potion, right?"

She drew her shoulders back. "One hundred percent certain I mixed it the way the family grimoire said to a 't'. If the potion and spell don't work, then it's wrong in the book."

"Have you tried any of the other potions or spells in the book?"

What if the book wasn't real? No, that wasn't right. Why would Saltine ask me to keep it safe if it wasn't real? She'd believed she was going to die. Dia, Father, and I had believed she'd died all those years ago. Who'd rescued her? I guess we'd never learn her story since she'd be long gone by now.

"I didn't." She bit her lip and stared at the glowing liquid. "I should have. We don't have time to head back and check another spell first. We need you to end your Trapper tracking spell as soon as possible."

"Relax, I won't turn into an evil monster."

She popped the cork of the tube. "Don't be so sure."

The liquid in the bottle hissed, and I raised a questioning eyebrow, but Pepper poured the liquid around the rat rock that was large enough that I could only see the top of her head over the mound. She returned to the start and sealed the line of the potion. The glowing green liquid stayed in its line as though painted onto the dirt.

Pepper searched in her pouch again and removed a folded piece of paper. She opened the edges and shook the creased page open.

"Once I break the magical barrier, do you think whoever is inside will attack?"

"I'll be ready." My hands glowed blue-green as flames flickered over them, then I called a sword of flames to my hand.

"Ah, that's very hot."

I laughed.

Pepper slapped a hand on her forehead.

"You're adorable," I said.

"Adorable?" She peered through her fingers then little by little lowered her hand. "If I'm adorable, then it makes you sweet."

I snorted.

"Exactly." She flicked the paper.

"Still adorable," I said. "When we've finished this, I intend to take you to a secluded spot and kiss you forever."

"Forever?" Her eyebrows rose.

"Aye."

"I assumed this was a fling. Scratch the itch where we were rubbing each other in irritation."

Her brows puckered adorably but a spark of hope lit her eyes. She might deny she wanted me forever, but it was there in the interest on her face.

"I will rub you in many ways forever."

She laughed. "You're such a rake. I don't know whether to take your words serious."

"I'll clear that up for you," I said, sending a surge of my power toward her as a warm breeze. It drifted over her cheek in a soft caress then over her lips.

Her body shuddered like it did when I kissed her, but now wasn't the time for kissing or showing her I meant forever. Dia, if only I hadn't wasted time holding onto a grudge that wasn't even warranted. Her lips parted as heat flared in her eyes.

"You're distracting me," she whispered.

"I wouldn't want to do that." I smirked.

"No." She wet her lips. "This is serious."

It was and I shouldn't be messing around right now, but I wanted her to keep looking at me the same way because once she watched me kill, she would be horrified. I gripped the flaming sword tighter in my hand and dropped the caress of wind from her lips.

"All right. Weave your magic."

Pepper nodded and read the spell.

"Magic woven,

Barrier before me,

Destiny calls,

For me to break.

Give me sight,

Reveal yourself,

In my name,

I call forth reality."

As she spoke, the words formed in the space in front of Pepper's mouth and floated in the air the same fluorescent green as the liquid. They circled the rock, hovered above it, then in a rush, slammed into the line of the potion. The potion exploded with a loud bang sending up a spray of dirt. When the dirt settled the glowing potion was no longer there.

She cocked her hip. "According to the book, the spell should have removed the magical barrier."

"Look," I said. "There's an entrance to a cave."

"So cool." Pepper grinned. "It worked."

"Now I go in."

"We go in," Pepper said.

"No, it's not safe for you."

"Stop arguing with me and wasting time. It's not safe for you since whoever is inside wants to kill Fae. Kill you."

"I can protect myself." I lifted the flaming sword and stepped toward the cave entrance. The mark on my hip flared. The potion still worked after all this time and now

I was certain I was dealing with a Trapper. "There's a Trapper inside."

"Shit. I'm coming with you then."

"Pepper."

"Save it, prince boy." She drew two potions from her pouch. "I'm not useless. I have potions that will help you."

"Prince boy?" I raised my eyebrows. "Your sassiness never stops, does it?"

"Nope and if you're planning on being with me forever, then you'd better get used to it." She lifted the vials. "Now, you lead the way with your glowing sword since that's an excellent source of light too."

"So now I'm a Fae torch?"

"You said it, not me." She smirked.

I shook my head. If she understood how much she meant to me, being my fated mate, then she'd tease me about it too. I almost wanted to tell her now, so I'd see her expression. So I'd shock her with the enormity of what she meant to me.

There was no way I'd deter the stubborn witch from coming inside the cave with me. I'd have to protect her from the Trapper too. I inched into the opening of the dark cave. The edges were rough in the rock as though chipped away by hand tools from eons ago. Inside, the opening was a long, jagged tunnel lit by my sword. I checked the ground and sides for traps, but there were none, which was unusual since magic had protected the entrance. Whatever was inside was important to a supernatural creature. A Trapper wouldn't have been able to place a magical barrier as strong as the one around this rock even if a witch had helped him. The force with which Pepper's magic destroyed the barrier told me it was someone with powerful magic who had put it here.

But who?

CHAPTER TWENTY-SIX
PEPPER

I DIDN'T LIKE THE cave. There was an inky sensation of evilness inside. I sensed other vibrations of magic too. What was with the barrier and this cave? Lorcan inched along the rough tunnel at such a snail's pace I wanted to shove past him and rush through it to get it over and done with.

Patience wasn't my strong suit.

Why had he said he wanted to be with me forever now? Of all the times to tell a woman, why did he choose this moment when we were walking towards an evil being intent on killing him? Did he think he wouldn't make it out alive? I wouldn't let that happen. My hands shook a little at the thought of Lorcan dying. My heart beat at a furious pace. Forever for a Fae was a lot different from forever was for me. I'd wither and die while he'd look the same all those long years and he would only die if someone evil murdered him with fire. Like those Trappers many centuries ago had slaughtered the Fae. But he could sense the Trapper. That would keep him safer than any other Fae, wouldn't it? The man was as good as impossible to kill.

But not entirely.

And now he was walking into a place we'd never been to an enemy who would kill him if they got a chance. I had to go with him. As strong as the Fae powers were, what would happen if the Trapper had set a trap Lorcan couldn't get out of? I'd never forgive myself if he died when I might have prevented it.

Each step deeper into the tunnel made the magical vibrations grow. Water dripped from the tunnel in long rivulets infusing the place with the scent of fresh water. The vibrations seemed to come from the water itself. I touched a finger to the wall and felt the magic of the water.

Lorcan snatched my hand away.

"What are you doing?"

"Trying to sense whose magic this is."

"And?"

"Someone a lot more powerful than a human Trapper used to live here," I whispered.

"Aye," Lorcan whispered back. "Do you sense any Fae magic in the water?"

I wriggled my hand from his grasp and placed it back in the water. The water tickled my finger. Vibrations hummed in the liquid, but they weren't anything like the way Lorcan's power felt nor his sister's powers.

"No. This is different, but I don't know who."

"Hmm." Lorcan looked at the water with a sad expression as though he'd hoped something connected the water to the Fae. "Did the Trapper kill them too?"

"I can only imagine they did."

We continued along the tunnel and the rough edges stopped and ended at a massive ballroom. Once it must have been grand, but now plants had overgrown the room. Tables and overturned chairs had become part of the landscape that nature had reclaimed in a twisted, macabre tale of destruction. On the stage at the end trees grew high to the ceiling that glowed with a luminous blue, every plant glowed the same color making the place even more magical.

"What is this place?" I whispered.

Lorcan stepped into the center of the room and spun around. "I'm not sure. It appears abandoned for a long time."

"The magic here tickles like raindrops on my cheeks."

"Hmm," he hummed. "What else do you sense?"

"Evil but it's not associated with the magic."

"Do you sense which direction?"

I nodded. "Follow me."

"I sense a Trapper too but it's faint and I can't figure out which direction to head." He grabbed my wrist. "Stay next to me."

"Okay." I clasped the vials tighter in my palms, ready to throw them when needed.

I led Lorcan across the ballroom. We dodged the fallen furniture and the plants that seemed to stretch toward us as though they hunted our touch. On the side, a wooden door sat. We opened it, and the cave morphed into a building made of brick. Wooden stairs led up and down, but the evil vibrations came from both directions.

"It's coming from both directions," I said.

"Let's head down first."

The stairs were only just wide enough for us to walk side by side. Each step made the sensation of evil grow thicker until I almost threw a potion to rid myself of the experience.

Lorcan's sword lit the way into the dark depths of the staircase. At the bottom of the stairs sat a large metal door appearing to lead to a vault. He tried the handle. It clicked open and Lorcan shoved the door on rusty hinges until the putrid odor of death and decay wafted to us.

I wrinkled my nose. "It smells like someone died in there."

"If I tell you to stay here, you wouldn't."

"No," I scoffed.

Lorcan sighed and stepped through the door. "Stay behind so I can swing my sword."

"Okay." I'd still have room to throw the potions from behind him.

We walked forward into the hallway of decay. Bars lined the right side and behind them were tiny cells separated by more bars.

"We're in a prison," I whispered.

"Dungeon," Lorcan whispered. "See the torture devices."

Now he'd pointed them out, I detected each cell had a set of shackles to hold the prisoner captive even further, and strapped to the walls were various instruments. I shivered despite the dungeon being warm.

I tapped Lorcan's shoulder. "This cell is where the sensation is the strongest."

Lorcan creaked open the door, but he didn't step inside. "It's empty."

"Look," I pointed.

On the filthy ground was a chunk of bloody flesh that was rotten and decayed.

"Do you think they're still being tortured?" I asked.

"No," Lorcan said. "If they were, then they'd still be in the cell."

"So where are they?"

"Who? The prisoner or the captor?"

"Both, I guess," I said. "I don't like this place. We should get back up."

"Who would be back up?" Lorcan asked. "I won't risk another Fae to a Trapper. And if there is no Trapper, then I won't have them fearing for their lives for nothing."

"What about the wolf shifters?"

"You heard Sledge, he's busy with a fire."

"But?"

"What if we leave and they realize we've been here? This is our chance to catch them by surprise. If they realize you've removed the protection barrier, they'll know someone is onto them. They'll run and we'll never find them," Lorcan said.

"You're right," I said. "I can't put the barrier back in place and once they realize we have compromised the cave entrance, then they'll hide somewhere else."

"We should check upstairs. Maybe there are clues," Lorcan said.

He led the way out of the dungeon, and I was glad to leave the place behind. If I ever saw a dungeon again, it'd be too soon. We walked back up the stairs and followed the next flight up toward daylight. Sunlight streamed in through windows on either side of the staircase and I peered outside at the rolling green hills.

"If I didn't know any better, I'd say we were in England," I commented.

Lorcan paused on the staircase and stared out of the window. "I'd say you're right."

"How is that possible? We walked into the cave in Australia. England is on the other side of the world."

"Magic," Lorcan said. "Powerful magic."

"Who has that much magic?"

"Fae can create such a thing. So can other beings."

"I haven't dealt with such powerful creatures. Even living in England I've never come across anything as powerful as you. Sure, there are wolf shifters like the traitor and I'm assuming this is how she met the man when he came out of the building here."

Lorcan placed a hand on the window. "Everyone went into hiding after the Trappers. I'm not surprised a witch as young as you haven't learned of the many creatures. Plus, you didn't have access to your family grimoire. You'll learn what you need in those pages."

"I read most of it," I said. "I'm looking forward to updating the family tree in the book."

"It stopped when Saltine handed it to me. I'm sorry I didn't give it back to your family sooner. I assumed they'd all died."

"Our family name is Willow. I guess Saltine changed it from Woodswillow." I shrugged. "It sure would be nice to learn why."

"None of your family know?"

"They haven't said and there's no one I could ask."

Lorcan dropped his hand and continued up the stairs. I followed behind him but the sensation of evil lessened. We came to the landing which opened into a mansion of decadent proportions, but dust covered every piece of furniture and floor except for the distinct track where a person had walked to the front door. As the only track the Trapper had walked, we stepped the same way slowly.

Outside the sky was a misty blue behind the stone-gray clouds. Even though the sun shone, rain was on the horizon. Rolling green hills dotted with thick green trees filled the landscape. I stepped outside and inhaled the cool air of my home country. Come to think of it, the countryside looked familiar.

"Holy moly," I said. "This place is near where I live."

"Here? Are you sure?" Lorcan opened the door and suddenly clutched his side. "I can sense the Trapper now."

CHAPTER TWENTY-SEVEN

LORCAN

"THIS IS NEAR YOUR home?"

"I can't be certain, but I think if we walked that way." She pointed. "For a few hours then yeah we'd be at my cottage."

"I don't like this." I frowned. "What if the Trapper knows about you and is waiting to kill you? And that's why he's outside here in England. He wouldn't venture out of the magical protection of the cave and this house unless he had to. He'd age each time he does. It would be why I never sensed him when I came to Earth. The timing would have to have been perfect for the potion to work."

"Don't be ridiculous," she said. "From what I've been told of the Trappers, they only care about Fae. And if this is near my home, then the entire countryside from my old hometown in Linton to the Bray Forest and beyond is under a protection spell so he'd still be under magic."

"This is too much of a coincidence, don't you think?" I ushered her back into the mansion. "I shouldn't have let you come."

"You didn't have a choice. I would have followed you."

"Next time I'll tie you up with vines."

Her face morphed into shock, then she blushed a pretty pink.

I let out a low chuckle. "Pepper, don't start thinking naughty thoughts now."

"I wasn't." She blushed even harder.

I brushed my knuckles over her cheek. "Sure, you weren't."

She lifted a challenging eyebrow.

"Whatever your heart desires, I'll give it to you, but not here. We need to head back so I can take you to Sledge's hotel where you'll be safe."

"How will I be safe at Sledge's?"

"You placed a protection spell around the hotel, remember? Plus, you'll have the protection of the wolf shifters."

"And who will protect you while you're out here hunting? Why don't you let me stay? We're here now. I know England and we're safer out here than in that cave we didn't know. Let's end this now."

She made a lot of good points. Should I risk her life to end the last Trapper?

"We shouldn't wait any longer with the blood magic in you." She crossed her arms over her chest. The potion vials glittered in the sunlight, snagging my attention. Pepper wasn't a defenseless mortal. She was a witch.

A potent witch from a powerful bloodline. She was stubborn too. I doubted I'd convince her to leave.

I sighed in defeat. "What potions do you have?"

She held up one hand. "This one stuns a person." She held up the other potion bottle. "This one creates a smokescreen."

"Can you put a protection spell on yourself?" I asked, with a sudden inspiration to keep her safer still.

"No, but I have a protection talisman." She dug into her pouch and lifted a bronze-colored pendant.

I stepped closer and cupped it in my hand. The intricate swirls of the metal were the same as the mark of the Fae mating mark. What were the odds?

"Where did you get this pendant?"

"I bought it at a flea market from a witch. She convinced me to buy it. Said something about it was fated to be mine. I liked it, so I bought it, plus she was very convincing."

"What did she look like?"

"It was hard to tell. She hid behind a thick cloak. Why?"

I ran a thumb over the pendant. "I wonder... Did she cackle a lot?"

Did Saltine foresee our meeting? Was it possible she was still alive too?

"She didn't stop once I bought the pendant and walked away. I turned around, but she'd disappeared into the shadows."

I laughed.

"What's so funny?"

"You met Saltine. She gave you the pendant."

"What! No way. Surely not..."

"I'd bet anything it was her."

"Why wouldn't she tell me who she was?" Pepper asked, a tinge of hurt coming through her voice.

"Saltine was always strange in what she did. I can't answer her why, but if she gave you the pendant, then it means she was alive recently and you might ask her yourself one day."

"It shouldn't be possible for Saltine to be alive this long."

"No," I said. "Neither should it be possible for a Trapper to be alive this long yet here we are."

Pepper stared at the pendant, and I pushed it back into her palm.

"If Saltine wanted you to have this, then you need to keep it close. She had visions of the future."

"So I've learned," Pepper ground out through her gritted teeth.

"Hey," I said, cupping her cheek. "It doesn't mean she doesn't want to know you."

"Right," Pepper drawled.

Behind us, the front door creaked open. I shoved Pepper behind me. How foolish to be standing around in the lion's den talking as though we weren't about to meet a monster. Pepper sucked in a breath, then gagged. The stench coming from the man was worse than death itself. My flaming sword seared hotter. Brighter.

"Filthy Fae," he spat through a mouth of blood-ridden spittle.

"Trapper," I said with the same amount of hostility.

"I'll end you all."

The Trapper smiled through his rotten face. Holes lined his cheeks leaving gaps to see into his cavernous mouth. His hair hung in clumps from his scalp as though he was melting. What he had left of his teeth were yellow and crooked. Behind him, he dragged a sword that appeared too heavy for the filthy man to lift on his rotten frame.

"I've waited a long time for this," the Trapper said, losing a tooth as he spoke.

"How are you still alive?"

His body twitched and a clump of flesh fell from his forearm onto the floor.

"They left me to rot like a corpse, but I escaped their cell. Idiots. All of you. You think you're so good with your magical powers. They should be ours. Humans rule the Earth, not you abominations. We should have your power. And it will be mine." He lunged forward, lifting the sword in a wide arc.

I met his swing with one of my own and landed my flaming sword on his normal sword. The two objects clanged on impact. Sparks flew and landed on the furniture beside us. The Trapper laughed and lunged for the door as though he'd escape me by heading outside. It wouldn't matter where he went, I'd find him now he no longer had the protection of the magical barrier around the cave.

Pepper's potion sailed by my head and with her perfect aim, it exploded on his back in a sparkling silver hue. He froze mid-lunge for the door. His face contorted into a sneer of pure evil, frozen for all time. I sliced his head from his body not wanting to see the reason for so many losses, the reason they had made me a killer. The reason I was a killer again. His head thudded to the ground and burst into flames. His body fell next and exploded in an even bigger fireball. The flames grew quickly, engulfing the door and the way out. It spread to the walls of the building so rapidly it was as though an accelerant ignited the fire into a blazing inferno.

Smoke billowed from the walls in an ever-increasing cloud making Pepper cough. I needed to end the fire now before it hurt her.

I drew my power back from the sword, and it disintegrated into nothing. My palms glowed as I used my magic and coaxed the wind to blow the fire away from her, but all my power did was make the fire bigger and fiercer. It should have worked. I should have forced the fire away from her. It was like the Trapper's body had acted as an accelerant. One that didn't want to be stopped. Pepper drew the edge of her cloak over her mouth and nose. She was struggling to breathe now and if I didn't end the fire, it would end her mortal life.

The flames spread to the staircase flickering up the stairs as though seeking Pepper on purpose. Every nerve in my body surged with panic. My stomach churned in fear I'd lose her. Drawing on the heavy rain clouds from outside, I sent a surge of rain to the flames closest to Pepper. The water hit the fire making it sizzle but instead of putting the fire out, it was as though I'd added more fuel to the flames. The fire roared so loudly, it drowned out the pounding of my heart beating wildly in my chest. I leaped toward Pepper through the flames, not caring they burned my skin. Every thought was for her. I had to get to her. Save her. I ran up the staircase and stopped before her.

"Why is my power not stopping the fire?"

"Magic," Pepper coughed and rummaged in her pouch. "He must have placed a curse on his body. Dammit, I brought no potions to counteract a curse."

Her breath came in wheezing gasps after she'd spoken, as though those words had taken a lot out of her. If I didn't do something soon, she'd die. My mate couldn't die. I'd only just found her. I could run through the flames and then I'd heal from the burns afterward, but Pepper didn't have supernatural healing abilities and burns would last a long time on her body. Burns might even kill her before I got her outside. If I stayed in the fire too long, I would die too.

"I'm sorry," I said, gathering her close in my arms because, through all my long years, I never imagined falling in love with a witch only to be useless in stopping her death.

"It's not your fault." She pressed her face into my chest. "I guess I'll die for a worthy cause."

"One Trapper isn't worth your life. Never. You mean too much to me." My hands flared with my power. "Hold on I'll try to smother it with a fire of my own. Fight fire with fire."

"Lorcan," she said with another cough. "If this was your idea of forever, then we need to have a serious talk about your version of time."

I choked on a laugh. "Forever means marking you as my mate."

She lifted her chin, her eyes glistened, but she smiled. "Do it."

"But it will kill you."

"We're about to die, anyway. Let me die knowing I meant something to someone."

My eyes welled with tears. Tears I hadn't shed for anyone in a long time. But this witch, she was my heart, my life, my love. How did she think she meant nothing to anyone? She meant the entire worth of my being. Every ounce of power in my body surged with the need to make her mine in the way of the Fae. I lowered her to the floor and placed one hand on her chest, the other I placed on the floor beside her, and I gave up the tight control I kept my power under. My hands glowed a luminous blue-green. Pepper's entire chest lit up with the abundance of magic surging into her mortal body. Her eyes widened not with pain but as though she was in euphoric bliss.

"Your power is so beautiful."

I gave her a sad smile. If this was it for us, then I would die happy in her arms. My power roared a fire from my other hand on the floor, it flared into a fire the same color as my power. Luminous flames merged with orange ones. I kept my gaze on Pepper's face.

Her beauty would be the last thing I saw before death claimed us. She was the only thing I wanted to see.

"Wait," Pepper said, her hand scrambling in her pouch.

"I can't hold it back."

The act of claiming her as my mate had sent my power raging with force, I could no sooner stop it than I could the fire.

She lifted the pendant and pressed it to my chest. I swallowed the lump in my throat.

"I want to give you a piece of me too," she rasped, then coughed again.

The metal heated and glowed against my chest. It seared my flesh through my shirt. Pepper gasped. My power slammed into her chest even harder weaving us together as mates.

"What's happening?" she asked as her eyes slammed shut.

"You're seeing all my memories. It's how Fae mark their mates. We share everything with them."

"If my head didn't hurt so much then I'd think this is cool."

"Don't worry," I said. "You'll fall asleep before the fire reaches us."

She moaned and clutched her head, then she slipped into unconsciousness so fast I was glad she wouldn't see her death by flames. The last thing she'd see would be my memories and my earlier memories were a happy time. She'd die happy. Knowing she meant so much to me. Knowing she was my fated mate.

The fire raged in a battle against my power. My mate lay at my feet in the Quiet as she absorbed my memories. It would kill her since she was mortal. No human had survived a Fae mating mark.

Placing both hands on the floor on either side of Pepper, I gazed at the peaceful expression on my mate's face. At least this way we'd die together. At least this way I'd never have to face the look of horror on her face when she witnessed all my dark memories.

I let out a roar of frustration and a surge of power so strong everything around me exploded in a fireball so enormous I was sure I'd blown the house to pieces.

CHAPTER TWENTY-EIGHT
PEPPER

WHERE THE HELL WAS I? A second ago, I was about to be burned to death, and now...

Now I was in a forest watching a little boy run between the trees. A girl chased him. They both had long silvery-blonde hair. The forest was gorgeous. Yellow leaves lined the forest floor while the tall white bark almost glistened under the bright sunshine. Their feet kicked up the leaves as they giggled.

"I'll catch you," the girl called.

"Never," the boy threw over his shoulder with a cheeky grin.

Wait! Was he a young Lorcan?

The scene flickered before me.

Young Lorcan sat on a boulder beside a running spring. An abundance of plants and flowers filled the space. It was so beautiful it made my eyes hurt.

"Lorcan, there you are," said a man with the same striking features as Lorcan. "Grandfather said you ran off instead of studying."

"What's the point of me learning how to become King? We're immortal."

"They can still kill us," Lorcan's father said.

"Who would kill Grandfather, you, and Rian for me to become King? It's pointless."

His father sighed and sat beside him. "I'll tell you a secret, but you must keep it between us."

Young Lorcan sat up and nodded his head. "I promise, Father."

"I don't want to be King either."

"You don't?" young Lorcan asked excitedly.

"I much prefer spending my time with my mate and my children." His father tickled him.

Lorcan rolled around on the ground kicking his legs and laughing.

"But as a royal Fae," his father said, "with a duty to our people, we're tasked with protecting our Spring of Life and we're tasked with leading them. It's an honor to be a royal. Embrace the honor, son."

"And if I don't?"

"I don't know." His father tugged him to his feet. "I'm happy and I want that for you."

"Do you think I'll find my fated mate one day?" young Lorcan asked.

"I hope so with all my heart."

Lorcan's eyes shone with sweet innocence. "I hope I do."

His father smiled kindly.

"I hope you do too, because the love I have for your mother is the best feeling in the realms." His father held out his hand. "Now, how about we head back to Grandfather's lesson?"

"Aye."

They walked from the atrium. I opened my mouth to tell them he had found his fated mate, but the words didn't come.

Scene after scene flickered in my mind. Lorcan with his mother listening as she sang. Lorcan at his study lessons with his grandfather. His grandmother taking him to Earth and showing him her power over lightning. His older sister Briana and Aislinn treating him like a child while his older brother Rian, always the studious obedient son, teaching him what he learned in the lessons. Then there was his sister Saoirse. They were so close and mischievous together.

So many happy memories filled my chest with warmth and love. The Summer Court was a beautiful place too. Every Fae was happy. They were kind and generous with their power. I watched him visit Earth and his mother's parents and extended family. Observed as the Fae wielded their powers to help the humans on Earth. Everyone lived in harmony. On and on the happy days filled my head. A permanent smile lit my face.

Then came the tragic day. I witnessed it all. The way Trappers burned his grandparents to ash on the stakes. Tears streamed down my face. After seeing the love they all had for each other, my heart broke into pieces. I'd never had the intense love of a large family like Lorcan, but I'd experienced it through his memories. And through his memories, I'd experienced the heart-wrenching loss too.

I gasped when I saw them visit Saltine that horrific night, all bloodied and bruised, giving Lorcan and his father the potions. Then I spotted the darkness overtaking Lorcan with every Trapper he killed.

So much blood and death. So many bodies. My stomach churned, but through it all, I noted the expression on Lorcan's face. The anger and need for revenge. Beneath those emotions was regret. Lorcan might have killed the Trappers, but he hadn't wanted to.

When he returned to the Summer Court, he confirmed my suspicion. He locked himself in his bedroom, curled into a ball, and cried himself to sleep. I longed to place my arms around him. Offer him the comfort he so obviously needed. Where was his family in his time of need? I wanted to run through the palace and demand they tend to him.

Everything changed after that night. One would expect no less, and my heart ached for the Fae. I wouldn't have comprehended the extent of the loss if I hadn't seen Lorcan's memories.

Watching Lorcan take Fae woman after Fae woman to bed made me curl my fists in jealousy. Was he chasing the elusive fated mate?

'I'm here,' I wanted to scream as I viewed each woman disappear into his bedroom. After each encounter, he'd lock himself in his bedroom and curl into a ball. No tears fell but the way he held himself said it all.

He would never have to feel that way again. He'd killed the last Trapper, hadn't he? I'd check the mark on his body as soon as I woke.

As I reached his memories of meeting me, I expected to wake up. I'd reached the end. This was it. I was Lorcan's, fated mate. He'd marked me. Claimed me as his in the way of the Fae. I'd open my eyes and look into his handsome face. Tell him he didn't need to look for love and acceptance as I loved him, accepted all of him, past and all.

The memory of the fire rose. The surrounding flames so close to our bodies, I understood my nightmare was true, and we hadn't made it out alive. There was no way we could have. The fire surrounding me was like my dream. I'd wondered if it was a premonition of my death.

Looked like it was for I didn't wake. Lorcan's memories returned to the start.

CHAPTER TWENTY-NINE
LORCAN

I WRENCHED IN A lungful of air, coughed, and inhaled again. Tiny particles of ash fell from my hand as it twitched beside my face. *What happened?* The fire. The surge of power. I sat up in a hurry.

Pepper!

She lay beside me. Still. As though dead. Ash and soot covered her in a gray blanket of filth. I brushed it from her face and placed a finger under her nose. Warm air brushed over my skin. She was alive! I sagged in relief.

How? How were we both alive?

I stared around the wrecked house. No walls were standing any longer. In their place was a pile of soot. The fire had burned so hot, it'd reduced everything to ash. So how were we alive when I'd destroyed everything around us? Was it the protection amulet Pepper had that was now seared into my flesh? Or was it my power? I brushed as much ash from Pepper as possible, then I gathered her into my arms and stood.

Which way? Green hills rolled in a gently undulating incline for as far as the horizon in the distance. Trees dotted the hills in a darker green but everywhere I looked was green with no sign of inhabitants in any direction.

There were no longer any stairs leading below. I must have incinerated the entire structure including the ballroom and dungeons below us. Which meant I wasn't able to go through the magical portal back to Australia and Sledge. I waved a hand, drawing on my power, and attempted to unlock the Veil, but try was the word. The Veil wouldn't budge for me. Even after Father locked the Veil, I'd never had it not open at all. Sure it was difficult, but going home always came easier than leaving the locked Summer Court. Never in my long life had I experienced the Veil keeping me out. What had happened? Why couldn't I unlock it now? Was it something I'd done? Or had Father changed the Veil yet again? No, I didn't believe he'd lock me out on purpose. Other magic must be in play right now.

"Dammit," I muttered.

Our Spring of Life might have healed Pepper now she wore my mating mark, and a Fae princess crown dotted her hair, but I wasn't able to get her to it. No one comprehended where I was. No one except Sledge, and he wouldn't find anything inside the cave now I'd destroyed it with my power. I cursed my stupidity of wanting to do this myself and not risk anyone else's life. What had I been thinking? If I'd traveled through the gate, then my destination would be on record. I'd have had guards with me. Guards who might have died fighting the Trapper. Except the Fae would think I was in Crystal Creek. It wouldn't have helped me as much as I believed.

The thick, heavy, gray clouds in the sky let loose raindrops onto our heads. I couldn't stay here in the ruins with no shelter for Pepper. I wouldn't suffer from the cold, but she would. Even though she was on death's door, I held onto the hope she'd live through my mating mark. Live to be with me. If I held onto that thought, then my fated mate was still here. Still a chance we'd be together. With a surge of determination, I tried accessing my powers again and reached for the Veil but only a small spark lit my hands. Perhaps I'd used too much to take down the cursed fire, and I needed to rest before I'd use it again, but it made little sense. We'd always had limitless power. It was why the Trappers sought to take our magic from us. My power was mine. No one could take it from me. The same way Pepper was mine. No one would take her from me either. I'd save her.

I stared at the wide-open countryside. In another time, another moment, I'd appreciate the beauty of the countryside. Not one building was in sight from the ruins, but Pepper said her home was within walking distance. I set off in the direction she'd pointed. Hope spurring me on. Hope and love. The rolling hills were like mountains on my tired body and heart, but holding Pepper close kept the thought of losing her for good at bay. The rain was driving sleet on my face and arms, so I angled Pepper's face to protect her more. I should have protected her better. I should have never let her follow me into the cave, but how was I meant to stop her when she was so determined? So strong-willed. Her breathing was deep and even as though she was merely sleeping. She was in the Quiet from my marking, but how long would she stay in it until her mortal body couldn't cope with my memories, nor the power of the Fae running through her body from the mark?

Each step took twice as long as I expected. I should have told her I loved her too. She deserved love, deserved to be told it, shown it, and I'd held myself back from telling her everything she meant to me. Regrets were hard to live with. I had plenty of them.

On and on I trekked as though each step would take me to a better time and place. Where Pepper would wake, and I could hear her voice once more. Would my family realize I was missing from the Summer Court soon? Time moved in a different way there to Earth so it might take a long time here before they came looking. And how would they find me? Earth was large. The only way would be if I was capable of taking us back to Australia. Perhaps I should have double-checked the stairs to make sure I'd reduced them to ashes, but they'd appeared destroyed from above. And I didn't want to leave Pepper alone and vulnerable while she was unconscious.

My mind wouldn't stop thinking of all the what ifs, of all the ways I could have done things differently. The rain smeared the gray soot on our clothes and bodies.

Pepper's cloak had taken the brunt of the ash and it protected her a fraction from the rain, but goose bumps had risen on the exposed skin of her limp arm. I adjusted her weight in my arms and drew the cloak around her body more. I could stop under a tree, shelter from the elements, and light a fire.

As the ideas circled my mind, I reached the peak of the next hill. Below sat a cottage. Smoke billowed from the chimney. A warm house would be better than sitting outside. I hoped whoever's house it was, they'd take us in. I almost ran down the hill, but I settled on a quick march. As I drew closer, I almost stumbled as Saltine's familiar cottage became clearer. How were we at her home?

I opened the tiny gate which was different to the gate I'd opened all those centuries ago. The front door flew open, and Saltine stood silhouetted by the lights inside. This time I stumbled, but I righted myself before I fell to my knees and carried on to the front door. I'd suspected she was still alive, but seeing her alive was still a shock to the system. She was a mortal witch. Was there more hope for Pepper than I first thought?

"How are you alive?" I asked.

"I could ask you the same," Saltine said. "Strip there. You're not bringing those filthy clothes into my home."

My eyebrows rose.

"The bath is full and waiting for you both." She turned her back and walked toward a large black cauldron sitting on the stovetop.

Dia, a hot bath would be perfect, and it would warm Pepper up quicker. I laid her on the stoop grateful for the shelter from the rain by the overhanging eaves and stripped my clothes. Next, I unclipped Pepper's cloak and stripped her clothes too. Saltine didn't even look our way once. She kept her attention on the cauldron and the liquid bubbling inside. Had she seen us coming with a vision? So many questions I wanted to ask her.

I scooped Pepper back up and walked inside, shutting the front door behind us.

"Don't take long cleaning up. There are fresh clothes in the bedroom for you both. Put her to bed, then come out here," Saltine said without even looking our way.

I nodded and walked into the bathroom I found through the open doorway. A large clawfoot tub sat in the middle of the room. Lavender-scented steam wafted from the surface of the water. Not letting go of Pepper, I stepped into the tub and sat down. The water was the perfect temperature. I longed to close my eyes and pretend everything was all right. That I was simply bathing with my mate, but heeding Saltine's words, I washed us both, then dried and dressed Pepper and placed her in the bed. I wanted to snuggle beside her under the crocheted blanket in a rainbow of blues. Instead, I dressed in pants and a shirt, noting the absence of the mark on my hip, and walked back into the other room.

Saltine peered up from the cauldron. "I see you've killed all the Trappers now."

My hand drifted to my hip. The small mark had disappeared, which meant I was no longer under a blood spell. No longer at the chance of becoming evil.

"Aye," I said stepping closer.

The cauldron bubbled a thick gray sludge. It smelled better than it looked.

"Did you see us coming?" I asked.

"I see a lot of things." She frowned and stirred the cauldron with a large wooden spoon.

"I'll take your answer as a yes." I leaned my hip against the counter. "Have you seen if Pepper will wake from my mating mark?"

"I can't say."

"Is there anything I can do to help her live?"

Saltine shrugged her shoulders.

"Saltine, please, if there is a spell, a potion, anything, tell me."

She turned and picked up a vial, then dipped it into the cauldron filling the small glass jar with the sludge.

"If she drinks this, then it will undo your mating mark. She'll wake at once."

"Give it to me."

"If you give it to Pepper, you'll never have the chance to mark her again. This potion will do more than remove your mating mark. It'll make her immune to your powers."

"I can live without my powers working on her so long as she's alive."

Saltine smiled and reached for a dagger on the table. Was she about to stab me?

"All you have to do to activate it is to add a drop of your blood."

My blood froze inside my body as my heart stuttered with her words. "Is it blood magic?"

"Powerful potions require powerful blood." She twirled the ruby-embedded handle of the dagger in her palm.

"But Pepper said blood magic turns people evil."

"She's right, and she's wrong. Blood magic opens a doorway for evil to come in. If a person is strong enough, evil won't make its way in," she said. "You didn't become evil."

I paced away from the cauldron. If I gave Pepper blood magic, was she strong enough to never turn evil?

"Is there a way to undo the potion if she turns evil?"

"Oh, yes, your death will do it."

I lifted the sludge-filled vial.

"Let me get this straight," I said. "I can give Pepper blood magic and she'll wake, be immune to my powers, but risk her succumbing to evil. If she does, then I'd have to die to stop her being evil."

"You summed it up."

"You have nothing easier?"

Saltine cackled. "You can wait and see if she wakes from your mark."

"But she's a witch and mortal. She'll die."

"Maybe. Maybe not. She has more than mortal blood in her body. There is a possibility she'll wake on her own accord."

Hope surged to every limb in my body but deflated in an instant. The weaker a person's power was, the longer they stayed in the Quiet. I didn't think Pepper was a weak person, but the amount of wolf-shifter blood she had in her made the chances of her waking almost nonexistent.

I lifted the vial and stared at the liquid. What would Pepper want me to do?

"What's your choice?" Saltine asked.

"I'm not sure. Pepper believes blood magic is evil."

"Why would she think that?"

"It was what the coven taught her. She'd hate for me to use it on her."

"It appears my lineage has a lot to learn. Have you passed on the grimoire?"

"I have." I nodded.

She twirled the dagger. "A drop of blood is all it will take. She'll be up talking to you in an instant."

I glanced toward the bedroom. Pepper didn't like the idea of me having blood magic in my system. She'd rushed to remove it from me fearing I'd turn evil. Pepper would hate to have blood magic in her. She'd hate for me to die so she would be free of evil.

"No," I said.

"Good choice." Saltine nodded.

I tossed the vial toward her. She caught it and dumped the contents into the cauldron. With a slash of her knife, she cut a branch of herbs hanging from the hooks behind her and tossed it into the cauldron. The sludge bubbled fast and turned white. The lavender scent surged into the air, and the liquid dissipated until there was nothing left so I couldn't change my mind even if I'd wanted to.

She stepped around the cauldron and air-kissed my cheeks. "Welcome to the family."

"Ah, thanks," I mumbled.

"My great, great, how many is it, Granddaughter has herself a worthy mate. Tell her I said so when she wakes."

"You said you didn't know if she'd wake."

"Oh, I knew. I had two visions though. Two futures. One where you chose the potion and one where you didn't. In both of them, she woke, but the outcome was different."

"How?"

"Does it matter now?"

"I suppose not, but I am curious... Did I make the right choice?"

"Time for me to leave." She flipped her hood over her head not answering my question.

"Wait." I grabbed her arm. "You're not staying."

"No. I can't stay. They'll find me if I stay here."

"Who will find you?"

"Don't you worry about that. I'll be fine." She tugged her arm out of my grasp. "Tell Pepper I wish I could have stayed. I would have loved to be acquainted with a powerful witch like her. Most of my offspring haven't known true love so I'm glad she has it with you."

Saltine walked toward the door. Black shadows formed around her body, and she disappeared before the door even opened. I blinked, trying to wrap my mind around how Saltine could still be alive after so many centuries when she was merely a witch. Or was she?

Her disembodied voice echoed inside the cottage, "Tell your mother it's almost time."

What did she mean?

She cackled and said, "And tell Aislinn her fate is in England."

I couldn't ask her what she meant with either of those comments for she'd vanished in a cloud of thick black shadows.

I strode back to the bedroom. Pepper lay on the enormous bed tucked under the blankets. Her beautiful face lay against the softness of the pillows. Her lashes lined her closed eyes. What I wouldn't give to have them open. To see her emotions flittering in the depths. Unable to stop from reaching for her, I stroked my hand over her cheek. She was warm to my touch, which had to be a good sign. Her breathing was even as though the fire and smoke hadn't damaged her lungs. The tiny flowers around her head were pale though. I sat on the side of the bed and held her hand in mine. A tiny flicker of my power surged. The mark from her talisman on my chest throbbed. I placed my other hand over the mark.

Were my powers tied to Pepper now?

Was she the reason they weren't working on the Veil?

Had I cursed myself to be powerless until Pepper woke?

If she woke.

I didn't care. I was powerless without my mate, anyway.

CHAPTER THIRTY

LORCAN

TIME PASSED. HOW LONG, I didn't know. I sat by Pepper's side. I massaged her body and moved her limbs hoping touch would wake her. She lay motionless. Expressionless. I missed her sassy remarks and the way she smiled. And I missed her moans of pleasure.

I missed her.

Perhaps I'd chosen wrong, and I should have woken her with the blood potion.

I tended the garden outside with my bare hands since my powers were still on the fritz. I had no way of returning to the Summer Court. No way of returning to Australia. No way of telling anyone where I was.

My family would be worried, and I hated I'd caused them stress.

I learned to cook food for myself the hard way. I'd burned the multiple recipes I found in the books on a shelf in the kitchen. Her notes on the pages made me feel like she was there with me cooking. The place might have been Saltine's all those years ago, but I suspected this was, in fact, Pepper's cottage now. Had someone handed the place down to Pepper from her family or was its mere coincidence she'd ended up in her family home? A cottage where I felt more at home every day. Every time I walked back through the front door, a cozy sitting room greeted me. A white couch with soft cushions I used to rest my head on and a thick, fluffy black blanket I covered myself with when I read one of the many books on witchcraft from her shelves. She'd written copious amounts of notes in the books and each comment gave me insight into the woman who was mine. Her intellect. Her humor. Her sass shone through in her words on the pages. Each word made me fall in love with her more. A brick fireplace sat opposite with a collection of candles in place of a pile of wood. Many nights I lit the candles and watched the flames flicker. Some nights I carried Pepper out to the living room and held her in my arms imagining her awake and talking to me. Other nights I lay in bed beside her, holding her close, wishing and waiting. Plants adorned her home and overflowed into the kitchen. Vines draped along the windows that looked out onto the garden which housed all her herbs. The cauldron was the focal point, but the white timber cupboards and the timber benchtops made it feel more like a home than a witch's spell room. Her bedroom was my favorite room though and not because Pepper was in it most of the time. She'd decorated one side of the room with a swinging chair made from macrame. Hanging plants trailed down the ropes holding the seat from the ceiling. Beside it sat a table with more candles and crystals that glowed when I lit the wicks. Often I'd sit in the chair and swing, watching Pepper as she remained in the Quiet absorbing my memories. Memories I'd never wanted to share with another, but I didn't care so long as Pepper woke.

One day, the flowers in her crown were a tad brighter. I almost imagined I was seeing things until the next day they appeared brighter still. I tried my powers and a little more energy than before surged into my hands.

"Pepper," I said. "If you can hear me wake up."

Her eyes remained closed.

Another length of time passed while each day the flowers grew brighter, more vibrant, like Pepper. My powers grew too. I connected with the Veil now, but I still couldn't unlock it.

What I'd been waiting for, for what felt like a lifetime, happened.

Pepper sat up in the bed and opened her eyes. "How did I get home?"

I dropped to my knees beside the bed and let out a sob. My heart throbbed back to life at hearing her speak at seeing her eyes open.

"Lorcan?" She scrambled from the bed and launched herself into my arms.

We rolled across the floor in a tangle of limbs as we held each other tight. I was too scared if I let her go, then she'd fall asleep again. Dampness through my top registered, and I tipped her chin back to see the tracks of tears on her cheeks.

"Why are you crying?" I asked.

She lifted a hand and brushed my cheek. "Why are you crying?"

I laughed and kissed her. For how could I not? My sassy witch was back.

We parted to take in a shuddering breath each.

"We almost died," she said.

"But we didn't." I brushed the hair back from her face and cupped her cheeks. "And you didn't die from my mating mark. It's a miracle."

"Just call me a miracle from now on."

"You're my miracle." I pressed a kiss on her lips. "Forever mine."

She lifted a hand against her chest and traced the swirl of my mating mark under her singlet. "I studied all your memories."

"I'm sorry," I said, my gaze dropped to the floor, so I didn't see the look of revulsion I was certain would be there.

"What are you sorry for?" she asked.

"You found my darkness. I never wanted you to see those scars."

She ducked her head until her beautiful face filled my vision.

"You're not the darkness. Lorcan, you're light and beautiful. You have love in your life, and you wanted to protect it. I noticed your struggles with what you did. The pain you suffered when you lost your grandparents almost broke me too."

"I loved them all so much."

"I saw," she said, sniffing back more tears.

She wriggled forward until she was sitting in my lap. My cock jumped to attention straight away. Pepper giggled as though my immediate response to her body amused her.

"How long have we been at my house?"

"A long time."

"Why?"

"My powers didn't work. I think they're connected to you now," I said, unbuttoning my shirt and showing her the burn mark from her talisman. "I'm uncertain, but I think your talisman and the mark it left have something to do with connecting my powers to you."

She gaped at the mark. "I'm not powerful."

"You're more powerful than you comprehend. No mortal has ever survived a Fae mating mark." I dropped my hands on her hips and stroked my fingers over the soft skin between her singlet and panties.

"I wonder how I did that?" She pouted in contemplation.

I leaned forward and sucked her bottom lip. She wriggled her hips, grinding herself on my hard cock.

"Are you trying to distract me?" I asked.

"From what?" She wriggled a bit more.

"From the fact you're awake. My powers should work, and I can take us back."

"Well, you promised to kiss me forever after we dealt with the Trapper." She scooted off my lap and bent over my raging cock, then she tugged my pants down.

"Dia, Pepper," I groaned with her face so close to me that I longed for Pepper to take me in the warmth of her mouth.

"The mark is gone. You're free from the blood spell. Thank goodness for that."

A small part of my brain registered I'd chosen right in not giving her the blood potion, but all my thoughts were on having my way with Pepper. Before I took over, she drew my hard cock from my pants and slid the length into her mouth. She moaned, sending vibrations along my shaft.

"Pepper." I moaned as she sucked my length until I didn't care about anything else in the world.

Her head bobbed up and down. Her tongue swirled into the slit of my cock. I couldn't move. She had me under her command. My miracle fated mate was awake and loving my body. My balls drew up tight. This wasn't right. I wanted her to experience pleasure too.

"Wait," I said, with more heat in it than I'd intended.

She lifted her head. "What's wrong?"

"Nothing. You're amazing, but I want to be inside you. I want to feel you coming on my cock when I come."

Her eyes darkened with lust. She lifted her singlet over her head and wriggled out of her panties. I'd wanted to undress her myself. Worship her body, but she appeared to be in a hurry. I stripped my clothes, and she crawled onto my lap.

"Let me touch you first."

"Lorcan, you've been massaging my muscles for who knows how long, I don't know about you, but I'm ready to explode."

"You sensed me touching you?"

"Yes." She clasped my cock in her hand and lined herself up. "I love you touching me. Touch me day and night forever. Sleep. Awake. Anytime."

The tip of my cock touched her soaking entrance.

"I would have given you many orgasms if I'd known," I said, placing my hands on her hips and urging her down.

She lowered herself, sliding her hot channel along my cock. The sense of completion made my eyes roll back in my head. She was slick and ready as she'd said. My perfect, strong mate, made for me and me alone as they made me for her. I'd love her forever and then some.

"I might have woken sooner," she teased.

"Don't worry," I said, rocking her hips back and forth with insistent fingers. "I'll wake you every day with an orgasm from now on."

"Promises, promises." She gasped as I picked up the pace and thrust with her.

"Oh, it's a promise. So were the vines."

Every promise I made was hers. Every touch was hers. From now on, she'd never have to wonder if she meant anything to anyone because I'd show her night and day. She shuddered. Her inner walls clamped around me, tightening on the sensitive head of my cock. It was so perfect being connected to her this intimately. As much as I wanted this to last, she was right. All the massages I'd given her while she'd been in the Quiet had inflamed my need for Pepper. Each rock of her hips as she worked herself on me brought me closer to the edge. My cock swelled. She moaned and so did I. We were so in sync. Her legs trembled and her pace slowed as she neared completion, but I kept going for the both of us. I'd always keep going for her. Just her.

A moment later her back bowed, and she threw her head back and screamed her pleasure as she came with a shuddering breath. Each contraction of her orgasm on my cock tightened until I came with her. Our gazes locked and held. Emotions flitted in the depths of her eyes. The same emotions I held for her and her alone. Our orgasms slowed, but the pounding of my heart didn't. It never would with my mate in my arms.

"I love you," I whispered.

"I love you, too," Pepper whispered back as though my words shocked her but made her happy she'd heard them.

My life was complete. My fated mate was alive. Marked. A miracle had happened, and I didn't know why or how, or who to thank but whoever fated Pepper to me, had chosen my perfect match. A mate I wanted to introduce to my family with pride.

"Ready to go to the Summer Court and meet my family?"

CHAPTER THIRTY-ONE
PEPPER

I'D CONVINCED LORCAN WE should spend the rest of the day pleasuring each other. Not that it took much convincing. A kiss was all it took, and he had me on my back screaming his name in pleasure. I'd never tire of his devotion to me as his mate to put my needs before others. Even his family. Even the world. I knew Lorcan would burn the world down instead of losing me and that was a heady knowledge to have about your mate. Especially when you'd seen him murder those who threatened his family and his people. Now I was one of those, but I was more than that to Lorcan. I was his fated mate. The one he'd choose before anyone else.

But I also understood how devoted he was to his family, so I relented and let us both get dressed.

Lorcan's power surged with a blue-green tinge as he reached for the Veil and unlocked it.

"Don't let go while we're inside," he said.

"What happens if I do?"

"You'll get lost in the Veil."

I stared at the swirling mist. I didn't want to get lost in the Veil. While the magic of the curtain between our realms was alluring, I suspected staying inside it wouldn't be pleasant.

"Okay." I placed my hand in his, knowing he'd keep me safe. Protect me from anything and anyone. "I hope your family will like me."

He smiled down at me with love shining clear across his face. "Expect them to take their time, but they will love you."

"I feel bad not telling Sledge we're okay first."

"Briana will tell him or Saoirse, or we'll go back and tell him. He's your family too. I wouldn't stop you from seeing him if that's what you want."

"I do, but we should see your family first. They'll be worried about you."

Lorcan nodded and drew me into the Veil. The mist swirled around my body and the view of Earth vanished. The Veil closed around us. Magic tingled my body. I stepped closer to Lorcan and hugged his arm. A moment later, a new image came into focus, and we stepped from the Veil into the atrium where their spring flowed.

"Lorcan!" Saoirse screamed so loud the entire palace must have overheard her.

She ran toward him and threw her arms around his neck. I let go of his hand, so he'd return her hug.

"Where have you..." Her gaze landed on me. "You mated."

"I did." Lorcan drew me to his side. "You remember Pepper."

"Of course." Saoirse eyed me.

I hadn't expected a warm welcome since I was a witch, but you'd think with her being mated to a wolf shifter she might be more accepting than the others.

"How did you realize he'd mated with me?" I asked.

Saoirse grinned. "Haven't you seen a mirror?"

"No."

She grabbed my hand and drew me toward the crystal-clear water. My reflection shone back at me like I was looking in a mirror. Flowers dotted my hair in the same way flowers crowned her head.

"I have a freaking Fae crown?" I exclaimed.

Saoirse laughed. "Aye."

I spun to Lorcan. "Does this make me a Fae Princess?"

He smirked. "Aye."

"Cool." I grinned. "I wish I had your powers too."

"Your magic is more than enough," Lorcan said.

"I think so too," Saoirse said. "I've learned about what you can do."

"Thanks," I said. Maybe she wasn't against me. She was probably shocked.

"So, you've seen Lorcan's memories?" she asked.

"Yes, why?"

"No doubt there will be a lot of jealous Fae women here when they learn of you. I was making sure you understood what was coming."

"I witnessed all of Lorcan's memories."

Lorcan grimaced. I stepped into his side and wrapped my arms around his waist.

"So, I understand I have nothing to be jealous of," I said. "Let them be jealous. He's my mate."

Saoirse grinned. "Now you're back, Father might stop having a fit. Mother too."

"Did he stop you from leaving again?" Lorcan asked.

"No. We've been back and forth many times since you disappeared. A lot of us have been searching Earth for you."

Lorcan's muscles tensed. Thank God we'd killed the last Trapper. If anything had happened to any Fae while they were searching for Lorcan he'd never forgive himself.

"Sorry," I said. "Lorcan stayed with me while I was in the Quiet."

"He should have brought you here. Anyway, we need to tell the others you're back so they can call off the search."

"Agreed," Lorcan said.

We walked out of the atrium and another blonde princess almost ran into us.

"Lorcan," Roisin said, throwing her arms around his neck. "Where were you?"

"Sorry, Roisin." He kissed her cheek. "I met my fated mate."

Roisin's eyes landed on me, then they spread into saucers. "She's not Fae."

"No, she's a witch. This is Pepper."

"Welcome, Pepper." She gave me a quick hug.

"Thanks."

"Everyone is finding their fated mate!" Roisin turned and skipped down the long marble hallway.

"She's cute," I said.

"Roisin is young," Lorcan said.

"She's not that young."

Saoirse and Lorcan peered down the hallway after her as though they were realizing the truth behind my words. We walked in the same direction as his sister. His mother rushed around the corner and skidded to a stop. Her breath stuttered in her chest, then she covered the remaining distance and hugged him.

"I was so worried." She squeezed him hard.

"Sorry, Mother. I returned as soon as possible," Lorcan said.

The Fae King rounded the corner next and took in the scene with a calculating eye. From Lorcan's memories replaying over and over in my mind, I'd learned a lot about this family. A lot about the King.

I stepped forward and held out my hand. "I'm Pepper, Lorcan's mate. Sorry it took me so long to wake after he marked me."

"She's a witch," Roisin said, skipping back around the corner, with more of the siblings behind her.

"I can see," the King said, taking my hand in a firm grip. "You remind me of someone."

"Saltine," Lorcan said stepping next to me. "She's related to Pepper. And Saltine is still alive."

"How?" Ciara asked. "Sorry, I'm Ciara."

"I'm Pepper," I said to Ciara, then turned to Lorcan. "You didn't tell me Saltine is still alive."

"She came to your cottage, which is Saltine's old cottage," Lorcan said. "I promise I'll tell you about it later. You distracted me from telling you earlier."

My cheeks warmed, and I squeezed Lorcan's hand.

"Sounds like you've had an interesting time," the Fae King said.

"I'll say. She told me to tell Mother it's almost time." He glanced at his mother. "What did she mean?"

Everyone stared at the Fae Queen.

Her lips snapped shut, and she flicked her gaze toward her mate. Whatever it was, she understood but she wouldn't say.

"I canna say," the Fae Queen said.

Lorcan turned to his sister Aislinn. "She also said to tell you your fate is in England."

"What does she mean?" Aislinn asked.

"I guess you'll have to go to England and find out, but we discovered a rumor Fae are living there. Maybe she meant you're the one who will find them," I said.

"Do you have the gift of premonition too?" Aislinn asked.

"Me? No." I shook my head.

Even though the dream I'd experienced for months had been a premonition of the night Lorcan and I almost died, I doubted with all my heart I would have more visions. Time would tell though, and I didn't want anyone to stare at me like I was a freak waiting for me to predict the future when I couldn't.

I was sure I couldn't.

Well almost sure.

Briana rushed into the cramped hallway and hugged Lorcan, then me.

"Can you tell Sledge I'm okay?" I asked.

"Who is Sledge?" the Fae King asked, staring at his daughter.

She lifted her shoulders and met his stare. "Sledge is my fated mate. He's the alpha of the wolf shifter pack where Arrow is from."

The King's mouth opened and then snapped shut. Shit, I'd forgotten Briana had told no one about Sledge and I'd just dumped her in it.

"Sorry," I mouthed in her direction.

"It was about time I told you all I have a mate."

The Fae King huffed. "And you'll live on Earth with him?"

"Sometimes, yes. I will live between both realms as I have been."

"Considering this news, I think it's time you brought your mate to meet your family," the Fae King said.

"Yes, Father," Briana said.

"Go to the doorway and take guards with you for Dia's sake."

"This hallway isn't the right place for all this," Mother said. "It's a splendid day. Let's head to the terrace for afternoon tea and become acquainted with Pepper."

This wasn't as bad as I assumed it would be.

"Lorcan," the Fae King said. "Can we have a private word?"

Maybe I spoke too soon?

CHAPTER THIRTY-TWO

LORCAN

FATHER WALKED WITH ME to the den. The place where all our secret conversations took place between the King and the princes of the family.

"I should tell Rian I'm safe," I said, opening the door and stepping inside.

"I'll send word to Rian and everyone else out searching for you. No doubt he will return as soon as he hears the news you have a mate," Father said, closing the door and locking it.

"Are you angry she's a witch?" I settled in a chair even though I was concerned he'd be upset.

Father sat and stared at me. I stared back expecting his crown to writhe in agitation, but it sat perfectly still on his head.

"No. We can't help who fate sends to us."

"I was so against witches I didn't even realize who she was to start with."

"And now?"

"Now I've seen how she'd give her life for mine—for the Fae. I'd never doubt her."

Father tilted his head. His crown of thorns swirled to life around his head, ruffling his hair in agitation.

"You can't make a statement like that and not tell me the details of how you came to this knowledge."

I sighed, realizing my mistake the moment the words had left my mouth.

"Father, I didn't want to worry you."

"Well, now I'm worried." He frowned.

I stood and paced the room. The King waited with the patience of a father who'd made mistakes and wasn't willing to make them again.

"You'll keep this to yourself?"

"You and I have always had our secrets, have we not?"

"Aye," I said. "Pepper and I learned there was a Trapper still alive."

"Impossible." Father stood. His power surged to his hands making the room glow a radiant silver.

"It's true. He'd hidden behind a magical barrier, so the potion Saltine made me didn't work until Pepper broke through it."

"She did that for us?"

"Aye. She followed me into the cave too. Into danger to protect me. I didn't want her to, but she wouldn't take no for an answer."

"What did you find in the cave?"

"There was a large ballroom at the end of the tunnel. Downstairs there were dungeons and upstairs was a mansion, but the mansion was in England, not Australia where we entered. Who has the power to make barriers and portal buildings?"

Father paced the room since I'd stopped to tell him what we'd found.

"It can't be..."

His steps tracked back and forth making a harried sound sending my nerves pulsing to the beats of his feet.

"What is it?"

He stopped and faced me. "Can you show me this place so I can be certain?"

"I incinerated the entire place when I killed the Trapper. I'm not one hundred percent certain but I believe my powers destroyed everything below too."

"Were there more Trappers?"

"No. He was the last one."

"How can you be sure if you didn't realize this one was still in existence?" Father threw his hands up in the air sending a flare of glowing power around the room.

"Because Saltine's potion put a mark on me and now it's gone."

"What mark? Why didn't you say you had a mark?"

I shrugged. "I believed it was a product of the potion, not a sign there were Trappers still alive."

Father sat back in the chair rubbing at his temples. I returned to my seat. I understood the way learning a Trapper was still alive made your head hurt. Made all the fear and pain come rushing back into your mind with a vengeance. How the images of losing loved ones made your heart ache. I also understood what he meant about having a fated mate taking away the pain. How the love and happiness you felt with your mate chased away the suffering. How Pepper had made me complete.

"The Trapper was rotten in flesh too. Whatever magic had kept him alive this long, it hadn't been kind to his body."

Father steepled his hands. "I know where he was, and I should have considered it sooner. This is my fault."

"What is?"

"The Water Sprites had a Trapper in their dungeons. I'd assumed Sir Axis had tortured him to death before that night. I should have checked."

"There weren't any Water Sprites in the place. It appeared whoever lived there had abandoned it a long time ago or they were dead."

"Sir Axis moved his people from the Everglades many centuries ago and took them into deeper hiding. He always used protection barriers, but he was paranoid that when the Trappers targeted us, they'd move on to them too. He must have left the Trapper in the dungeon and figured he'd die."

"But the magic kept him alive all this time." I blew my breath out through my teeth.

"How did he escape the dungeon?"

"I'm not sure, but Pepper said the magic protecting the entrance had weakened over time. That the maker hadn't kept the spell up to date. Perhaps this also weakened the magic in the cells enough that he could escape?"

"It's still a guess," Father said. "We'd have to ask Sir Axis if he left the Trapper alive, but who knows where he's hiding his people now."

"Everyone seems to hide. Perhaps it's time we stopped. Look how many of us have found our fated mates coming out of hiding. How many of us are happy now."

"I'm glad to hear you're happy with your mate." He smiled.

Returning his smile, I said, "Pepper is special, and I am so happy with her."

"She must be to survive a Fae mating mark as a witch. I'm looking forward to getting to know her."

He stood and the power in his hands diminished to nothing once more leaving the room absent of the silver glow. I understood the need to keep certain secrets with your mate. I stood and opened the door. We walked along the marble hallways until we came to the terrace. Pepper sat on a chair, sipping tea from a dainty cup. In her other hand she held a square of orange cake. She smiled sweetly at my family, who were talking with her in animated conversation.

I stood behind her and placed my hands on her shoulders unable to keep myself from touching her.

"Everything all right?" she asked, tilting her chin up.

"Aye. Perfect. And you?"

"I'm good. I saw how wonderful your family is from your memories. It's like I know them already." She lifted the cake toward her lips and smiled. "Plus, the Fae bake delicious sweets. I could get used to the Summer Court."

"It's up to you where you want to live." I rubbed her shoulders.

"Let's take one day at a time. Besides, with your cool power and this Veil travel, we can go anywhere in the world in a moment."

"Any country, any realm so long as I'm with you."

She kissed my knuckles with the barest of brushes of her lips that I felt in my heart.

Aislinn leaned forward. "Where do I look for the Fae in England?"

It was the first time I'd seen anything other than anger in her eyes for a very long time. Had my sister changed so much seeing me find my fated mate?

Pepper leaned closer. "I have a few contacts in England we can ask." She turned her head over her shoulder and smiled. "We're heading back to England first."

"I wouldn't mind visiting your cottage again," I said with a wink.

Pepper blushed a pretty pink, making me want to take her back there now, but right this second, my family was interested in talking with Pepper. I wouldn't take this moment of having a family away from her. She deserved all the love in the realms. And I'd make certain she'd have it every day of her now immortal life.

BONUS SCENE

Download your free bonus scene from Fae's Witch.

Fated Mates of the Fae Royals

1. Fae's Song

2. Fae's Wolf

3. Fae's Alpha

4. Fae's Heart

5. Fae's Witch

6. Fae's Dream

7. Fae's Fate

8. Fae's Love

ACKNOWLEDGMENTS

First, thank you to my family for putting up with me disappearing into the world of books. A special thank you to my daughter Sarah for designing my beautiful covers. To Belinda, thank you for encouraging me to write again after I lost everything in a computer crash. Remember to back up! A lot of work goes into creating a story, and I'm always thankful for the support of my online writing buddies, beta readers, and fellow authors, Immy for always making me smile, Tammy for believing in me from the start, Karen for being willing to read any level of heat I write, Cassie for her hand holding, Lana for her invaluable knowledge. The biggest thank you goes to my 'twin' Dannielle, who is the best critique partner, cheerleader, and sounding board ever, and is forever fixing my comma errors, sorry Dannielle I'm afraid you're stuck with them and me. Finally thank you to all you romance readers. You are my tribe.

ALSO BY

FANTASY AND PARANORMAL ROMANCE

Summer Court

Fae's Song

Fae's Wolf

Fae's Alpha

Fae's Heart

Fae's Witch

Fae's Dream

Fae's Fate

Fae's Love

CONTEMPORARY ROMANCE
Billionaires' Reluctant Brides

Their Love Deal

His Pleasure Contract

Love Negotiations

Her Love Submission

Hollywood Hearts Short Stories

How The Grinch Lusted After Santa

Lusting After Valentine

The Lustful Leprechaun

The Lust Bunny

Lustman To The Rescue

The Lust Giving

Hope Bay

Moving On With Mr. Fix It

Falling For Mr. Faking It

Anthologies

Reluctant Bride

Alpha Male

ABOUT AUTHOR

Helen Walton is a tea drinking, chocoholic, romance writer. Stories are her obsession. She adores creating sensual romances containing a sprinkling of humor and the all-important happy ending. She lives in South Australia with her family, and menagerie of quirky animals where they all take her away from her book world and demand to be fed. Lucky for them, she enjoys cooking but prefers baking.

Sign up for my newsletter for exclusive content.

https://www.helenwaltonauthor.com/newsletter

Visit my website

https://www.helenwaltonauthor.com/

Follow me

BB bookbub.com/profile/helen-walton

f facebook.com/Helen-Walton-Author-1034966677
06602/

g goodreads.com/author/show/20249188.Helen_Wa
lton

instagram.com/helen.walton.author

tiktok.com/@helen.walton.author